Also by

Shannon Esposito

SAHARA'S SONG

STRANGE NEW FEET

THE MONARCH

KARMA'S A BITCH

LADY LUCK RUNS OUT

Silence Is Golden

(A Pet Psychic Mystery No.3)

A NOVEL

Shannon Esposito

misterio press

Silence Is Golden
(A Pet Psychic Mystery No.3)

Copyright © Shannon Esposito, 2013
Published by misterio press

Printed in The United States of America

*****

Visit Shannon Esposito's official website at
www.murderinparadise.com

*****

Cover Art by India Drummond
Indiadrummond.com

Formatting by Debora Lewis
arenapublishing.org

*****

ISBN-13: 978-0-9913208-2-0

Dedicated to my golden girl, Rainey.

CHAPTER ONE

Does everyone in St. Pete have a secret? That was the question foremost in Victoria's mind during her run. She had discovered two shocking secrets in the past week alone. One she would keep. The other she couldn't. Checking her watch as she and Goldie stopped in front of Fresco's Waterfront Bistro, she fought to steady her breath from the three-mile jog and smiled down at her panting golden retriever. "We made good time, girl."

Pulling the backpack off her shoulder, she pushed aside the secrets for now and rifled through it with a sense of well being. She was finally taking care of herself, and it was paying off. At forty-five she was in better shape than she had been in her twenties when she first married Eugene. If only she could go back in time and tell her naive, meek self how it would turn out. So much of her life and energy had been spent trying to be enough for him. She still loved him, but he wasn't her priority any longer. Taking care of herself and Goldie, that was her focus now. Time has a way of making you sort out your priorities. Especially after a death.

Locating the water and portable dog bowl, she poured just a few mouthfuls.

Her three-year-old golden retriever sat obediently, tongue lolling, bright eyes sparkling as she waited.

"Here you go."

Goldie stuck her snout in the bowl and lapped up the water, licking the bowl dry and then grinning up at her with foam and drool dripping from her chin.

Victoria chuckled and took a long pull from the water bottle herself, then stuffed it—and the bowl—back in her pack. She scratched the dog under her wet chin.

"You can have more after you cool down. Come on, baby girl."

She still had about twenty minutes before Jade would be meeting her. Wiping at the sweat dripping down her face, she felt her heart skip. She couldn't wait to see the look on Jade's face when she showed her what she'd found in her late Uncle Renny's attic. *Why didn't he leave any instructions for what to do with it?* She supposed it didn't matter. Jade would be the one he'd want to have it. It wasn't like he tried to hide the fact Jade Harjo was the love of his life. Well, at least after Auntie Harriet died he didn't. Before her death, it was the secret everyone pretended not to know about, even Aunt Harriet. The skeleton in their family closet. Anyway, Jade would have to be careful with the artifact and who she showed it to. Would she give it to the museum? Keep it hidden like Uncle Renny did?

A soft *woof!* came from Goldie as she walked glued to Victoria's side, head up, sniffing the salty evening air.

Victoria startled and glanced around. "What is it, girl?"

There was no movement she could see. Dusk was settling. This was usually her favorite time of day but even as her breathing and heart rate returned to normal, anxiety tightened her gut. She mentally dug around, trying to find its source, but couldn't pinpoint it. Shaking it off, she continued to lead Goldie along the strip of parking lot between 2nd Avenue and the boats docked in the bay. The slapping of water against the boat hulls was hypnotic, and she let herself be soothed by the sound. The dusty purple and orange sunset had morphed into a smoky gray sky.

Why hadn't she and Eugene ever bought a boat? Goldie loved the water. She'd have to talk to Eugene about that. She knew nothing about boats. She sighed. If he ever spoke to her again. Oh, who was she kidding? He'd be angry for awhile and then they would make up. They always did. At least she had this. This predictability in their relationship. She was doing the right thing, and he'd just have to get over it.

Car lights swooped over them as someone turned onto the strip of blacktop. Victoria steered Goldie to the side, moving into the parking spaces, closer to the boats. She eyed a white boat. Even without the sails raised on the poles, it was an elegant creation. She could picture herself, Eugene and Goldie lounging in the middle of the bay in a sailboat. Yeah, that'd be nice. It would give them something to do as a family, too. Something in common.

The car's engine spun loudly. Glancing back, irritation stirred in her chest. She squinted into the headlights. Why was the driver going so fast? What a jerk. This was a parking lot, not a speedway for crying out loud. She pulled Goldie deeper into the empty parking spaces to give this idiot plenty of room.

Her next glance back threw her heart into her throat as the headlights blinded her. She screamed. A loud thud burst in her head. Helpless, she tumbled over the hood and smashed into the windshield. Then the pavement came at her at blinding speed, cracking her skull, her shoulder and legs as she tumbled across it like a rag doll.

The world had gone silent. Her head pounded in that silence like a far off drum. Tiny shells and pebbles from the pavement pressed into her right cheek. As she listened to her own shallow, rattling breath, she watched the car turn around and stop in front of her. The door swung open. Lights so bright. Black heels and familiar legs stepped out, stumbled and then ran toward her. She shifted her eyes. They were the only thing she could move. Where was Goldie? *Goldie!* A sob stuck in her throat. She wanted to scream, *Find Goldie! Why would you do this?* No sound would come. Her eyelids fluttered. So heavy. An eerie peace settled over her like a warm blanket, taking away all feeling in her body as she sank into the darkness.

CHAPTER TWO

I leaned against the crow's nest railing of the 70-foot pirate ship, enjoying the rush of cool air over my face and gazing at the wedding party dancing the Macarena on the deck below. They were all decked out in pirate outfits, except for the bride, who twirled and stepped along despite being in a floor-length, sparkly white gown. I chuckled as I noticed her tiara had been replaced by a pirate hat. From princess to pirate bride, now that's a good day. Between the hum of the engine and the loud music, I felt immersed in the small space and celebration, and my heart was just bursting with all the happiness buzzing around me.

"What do ye say, me beauty? Wanna dance with this ol' land lubber?" Will growled into my ear. His body was pressed against mine, one hand on either side of the railing. I felt protected from the chill of the February night air and content to be right where I was, enfolded in his arms.

"You're so sexy when you talk pirate." I chuckled. "Maybe if they play something slower." Between the champagne that had flowed in plastic cups after the ceremony and the motion of the ship, I was sure attempting the Macarena—a dance

I had never learned—would leave someone with bruised toes... or me with a bruised ego.

When Will first asked me to be his date for his co-worker's wedding on Captain Memo's Pirate Ship, I thought he was joking. Turned out, nope. Real pirate ship, real wedding. But, I have to say, so far it has been an evening I won't soon forget. Not to mention the first wedding I've ever been to. Our family back in Savannah didn't get invited to many social events. As in none. Ever. But, moving to St. Pete last summer has given me an opportunity to make up for lost time. There's always somebody celebrating something in this town.

As the song ended, I noticed the ship was turning, getting ready to make the return trip back to the marina. I sighed, moving my attention from the wedding party to the horizon. I didn't want this night to end. The brilliant gold sunset, that everyone had paused to snap pictures of, had given way to a purple-hued sky with just a touch of pink left of the show. I was surprised at how close we had stayed to land. It was now a swath of green between the darkening sky and gray water, the rows of rectangular buildings lit up like a string of white Christmas lights along the coast.

The sound of bells being struck twice rang through the air, bringing my attention back to the ship. That was the signal for us to cover our ears, so we did. Whistles erupted as one of the pirate crew brought out a small, hand-held canon. We could see people waving from the St. Pete pier. Everyone shouted back as they held their hands over their ears. *Boom!* The canon spit smoke that billowed up from the deck and then quickly got swept away. Everyone cheered and another song with a heavy beat sent the partygoers into fits of dancing once again.

Will snuggled his nose into my neck and pressed his body against me. "You smell good."

"You feel good." I smiled. My gaze fluttered and then narrowed as something in the water between us and shore caught my eye. Small splashes were breaking the surface. I leaned further over the railing. *Maybe a pelican in distress?* It was only about thirty yards away from us, but the fading light made it hard to make out details.

"What is that?" I pointed. Will leaned further over, narrowing his eyes at the disturbance in the water. We were both silent as we watched.

"I can't tell. I don't think it's a person, looks too small. Maybe some kind of big fish that's injured?"

"I'd bet my bottom dollar the captain has binoculars."

Will kissed the top of my head and sighed. "Let's go ask." He knew by now my curiosity always got the best of me and so we made our way down the stairs, through the crowd of dancers and up two more flights of stairs to the captain's deck.

"'Excuse me, Captain," Will said. "Would you happen to have a pair of binoculars we could borrow?"

"Aye!" The captain smiled, staying in character. "That I would, Matey." He reached down into the wood shelves below the wheel and handed them to Will. As Will adjusted them, the captain asked, "Dolphins?"

"Not sure."

The captain smiled at me, his cheeks flushed, his eyes gleaming, obviously enjoying his work. "Having a good time, Lassie?"

I nodded. "Yes, thank you. Great ship you've got here."

"Aye, She's a beaut, she is."

Will pulled his eyes away from the binoculars, frowned and handed them to me. "Darwin, take a look and tell me what you think it is."

Shoving them against my eyes, I scanned the water until I found the disturbance and it felt like the world stopped. "Oh heavens! Will, I think that's a dog!"

"That's what I think, too."

"A dog?" The captain's smile and pirate accent disappeared. I nodded and handed him the binoculars. "Well, I'll be—"

"We have to help him or he's going to drown out there. Can we get closer?" I crossed my arms over my chest as my heart began to flutter with anxiety.

The captain glanced up at me, his brows pressed down with concern, and then he grabbed the wheel. "I have a bunch of animal lovers on my crew. Don't think they'd forgive me if I didn't."

He powered the ship down. It cut smoothly through the water as he brought it back around towards the dog. Then he took another peek through the binoculars. "Though, not sure we'll reach him in time. Looks like his head is going under." He stopped the music and called out over the loudspeaker. "Man overboard!"

I watched, fascinated, as the crew below us sprang into action. Two pirate women emerged quickly with life rings while two others herded the wedding party and guests away from the swinging door on the side of the ship that would give them access to the water. A life raft was quickly shuttled to that door.

"What's a dog doing that far away from land?" Will shook his head and scanned the surrounding water. "I don't see any boats around that he could have fallen from."

"Don't know but here's the catch." The captain glanced up at Will, worry now pinching the corners of his eyes. "We aren't allowed to actually get in the water, per Coast Guard regulations. Usually with humans, that's not a problem. We deploy the life raft, they get in and we pull 'em to safety. With a dog? Not sure how we're going to get that critter on the raft."

Will held up his hand. "Say no more." He motioned for me to follow him, and we made our way quickly back down the stairs to the crew members holding the raft.

"Sir, we need you to go to the other side of the ship." A worried crew member stopped him. The others were scanning the water in confusion.

Will kept his voice calm but urgent. "The captain has told me about your regulations concerning rescue. This isn't a human overboard, it's a dog. The only way to save it is for me to go out there in the raft. You're not allowed, I understand, but there's nothing stopping me."

She shared a confused glance with her coworker, and they both scanned the water further out until they saw the distressed animal.

"Oh!" she said in surprise. Turning back to Will, she nodded and they lowered the raft into the water. Will removed his jacket, shoes and watch, handing them to me.

"Hurry," I said. We were close enough now that I could see the dog's head disappearing beneath the surface. His energy was depleted. We weren't going to reach him in time.

There was only one thing to do.

As Will climbed down into the raft, I closed my eyes and steadied my breathing, following the salty air in and out of my lungs and moving my attention to the place where I could connect with the water. When I reached my center and felt my mind flow in sync with the water, I opened my eyes and concentrated on the area around the dog. Gathering the water around it and beneath it, like a cradle, I watched the dog's body bob up to the surface. Then I pulled the water toward us with everything I had. The boat rocked gently.

Come on, boy. Just hang on a little bit longer. I pulled back slowly, being mindful to concentrate on keeping his head above the surface. Energy dissipated from me at an alarming pace.

I had been practicing, doing small exercises since I had decided it was irresponsible to shun my gift, but this was my first big test of control. My legs felt heavy and began to tremble. I held on tighter to the edge of the ship for support and made an effort to refocus. A surge of energy flowed out of me. Fifteen feet. We could see him clearly now, floating limp, barely treading with his front legs. Ten. My eyes watered with the effort and the wind. The crew had gathered around us, their voices escalating as the gap between Will and the dog closed. Five feet.

The light had faded fast. The captain shined a powerful flashlight on the dog as Will used his hands to paddle toward it. Almost there.

When Will slipped his arms underneath the soggy, limp animal and dragged it onto the raft, cheers erupted around me. I collapsed against the railing, pulling my energy back inward to feed my exhausted mind and body. Will's phone buzzed in his jacket at my feet.

Leave a message. He's kind of busy at the moment.

The crew hurried blankets over as Will cradled the wet, shaking dog in his arms. I grabbed a blanket and wrapped it around Will's shoulders while someone wrapped another one around the dog.

"He's alive. That's a miracle. Any tags?" I asked, gently drying its head with a corner, being careful not to make contact here in front of all these people. A dog in the middle of the Bay had surely suffered some trauma. I needed to get the dog alone to find out what happened, and see if we could get him back to his owner.

"Nope. No collar. It's okay now, you're safe," Will cooed to the dog as he joined me in rubbing it with the blanket. I was grateful for the bodies gathered around us as they blocked the wind.

Some of Will's police pals, giddy from the rescue and all the champagne, were already giving him a hard time about being a hero. He tried to act annoyed but I could tell he was happy this little guy was okay.

"It's a golden retriever," I said to Will. "Looks well taken care of. Somebody's gotta be missing it." The poor thing was panting and shaking, the whites of its eyes showing as it gazed off in shock. But it was alive. I briefly glanced up and thanked the stars for that.

Will carefully checked each of its legs for injury, moving each one slowly. No yelping. That was a good sign. I watched him move his hands along the dog's body under the blanket. A little flinch.

"Might have a sore rib, but I don't think it's broken." He looked up at a pirate lady. "Let's get him some fresh water." Then he continued gently rubbing the dog's ears and neck with the blanket. He sighed and pulled the blanket tighter around his shoulders. "Darwin, can you find my phone? We'll get him to the emergency vet after we dock. I'll let them know we're coming."

I nodded and went to retrieve his things.

When I handed him the phone, he glanced at it and visibly stiffened. As the dog greedily lapped at the fresh water he was given, Will listened to a message and dialed a number. But, it wasn't the emergency vet he was calling. He was the homicide detective on call, and a body had been found.

CHAPTER THREE

While Will struggled to change quickly into a dry pair of clothes from the trunk of his car, I took the opportunity to finally be alone with the dog.

Will had carried her—we'd discovered it was a female—through the parking lot back to his car and laid her on the blanket in the backseat. I knelt down in front of the open door now and looked into her scared, brown eyes. My heart twisted in my chest.

"Okay, girl, let's see what you have to tell me about your little evening swim." Taking a deep breath, I exhaled and rested my palms gently on either side of her head.

Zap! A force hit me like I had just bounced off a brick wall. I raised an arm to my face as blinding white light assaulted my senses. An impact like a bomb exploded in my head. The world spun as I tumbled. Panic. A sweet smell. Lilacs? The need to run consumed me. *Splash*! Cold water surrounded me.

I fell back on my bottom and immediately jumped back up and jogged away from the dog so I wouldn't startle her. *Shoot. Jumping jacks weren't helping.* My skull throbbed from the energy building inside my head. I took off, sprinting back and forth in front of the car. After about the tenth lap, I felt the energy disperse. *Pop!* As I collapsed on the ground, a street light overloaded above me and blew out.

Well, I patted myself on the back, that wasn't too bad.

"Darwin?" Will stood by the open driver's door. While he slipped into a dry jacket, he stared at me with one eyebrow raised. "You okay?"

I pushed myself off the ground, dusting off the new pale yellow pantsuit that Sylvia—my friend and business partner at Darwin's Pet Boutique—had helped me pick out for the wedding. My cheeks burned. "Yep, hunky-dory. I'll explain in the car."

I slipped into the back seat of the sedan and snuggled up next to the dog. "Okay, girl. We're gonna do everything in our power to find your family, don't you worry." As I tucked the blanket around her, she plopped her head down in my lap. Her body was stiff, and she was still trembling. I cracked a window to try and lessen the wet dog smell permeating the car.

Will flipped the siren and lights on to push through the Saturday evening traffic which, it turned out, was a nightmare.

"Come on, move it," he grumbled.

The more time I spent around him while he did his job, the more I admired him. I mean, yeah, I was all for needing justice and doing some amateur sleuthing when it was necessary, but every part of Will's job was a challenge to say the least. From solving a murder to just getting to the crime scene.

Crossing the packed bridge was really slowing us down. He glanced in the rearview mirror as he expertly maneuvered around the cars trying to squeeze over to the side. "So, what happened back there?"

Oh. Yeah that. I bit down on my lip. "Well, remember how I told you I get visions from animals that have suffered recent trauma?"

I saw Will's knuckles go white as he gripped the steering wheel harder. "Yeah?"

I ignored the fact he still wasn't comfortable with my psychic abilities. "Well, the information I get from them comes in the form of energy. Negative energy that is usually pretty strong. So, I have to purge that energy after the vision. Get it out of my body in a controlled manner. Otherwise bad things happen."

His eyes flicked back to me in the mirror. "That's what all the running around was?"

"Yeah." I frowned. I could only imagine how ridiculous I had looked. "Usually it's light bulbs that absorb the energy and burst."

"Wait—" Will's eyes narrowed. "That time we found Karma with Mad Dog at the lake... the cruiser headlights blew out. That was you?"

"Yeah. Sorry."

"Huh." He was silent for a moment and then nodded. "So you got a vision from this dog, too?"

My hopes soared that he was accepting my gift. Plus, I had no prior knowledge of this dog, so if I could give him information that proves I received a vision from her, then he would have no choice but to believe me. This could be a blessing in disguise.

"Yeah, I got some information from her. She hit something hard. Probably why her ribs are sore. There was a sweet perfume smell present, like flowers. Lilacs. Lots of panic. Oh, and a blinding white light. She felt the need to run. Then she was in the water."

"Interesting. Not much to go on to find her owners, though."

"No." I shrugged. "Not much this time." We finally pushed out onto the highway, and I felt the pull of the sedan speeding up. "So, do you get called to every death in the area?"

Will glanced at me in the rearview mirror as he sped along I-275. "When I'm on call, yes. Homicides and accidents that could be homicides. We treat hit and runs like a homicide until we can prove otherwise. That's what this one looks like. A hit and run."

"So sad. Will you be there awhile then?"

"Yeah. I'm sorry. I'll see if I can get someone to drive you two to the emergency vet after I assess the situation."

I ran a hand over the dog's damp, floppy ear. She glanced at me sideways, the whites of her eyes showing. "You're safe, baby," I cooed. Then to Will, "That's okay. I can call a cab."

We sped off the exit ramp and down 2nd Avenue toward The Pier. As we crossed Bay Shore Drive, Will made a sharp right into the marina parking lot. Blue lights were flashing off the line of boats at the water's edge. Emergency vehicles filled the narrow lot. He pulled up right beside the yellow crime scene tape barrier. "Stay here. I'll be back in a minute."

I rolled the window down all the way and watched him walk a few feet to the policeman standing in front of the tape. He handed Will some kind of clip board, and Will scribbled on it.

"What do we have?" His voice carried on the crisp night air.

"Female victim, DOA. ID... forty-five." I could only hear snippets of his side of the conversation.

Will's hands were on his hips. "Coroner notified?"

"Yes, sir. He's on the way."

I strained to see around the ambulance to where all the activity seemed to be. Camera flashes were going off. Will glanced back at me and then stepped under the tape. I sighed and settled back into the seat.

Glancing down, my heart sank. Blood had seeped through the blanket. I lifted the blanket carefully off the dog's hip. Yep, the wet fur was matted with blood. Her jagged breathing showed no sign of calming down. She was probably in shock.

"All right, girl. Time to get you to the vet." Digging through my straw bag, I found my phone and dialed the Emergency Vet Clinic to let them know we were coming and then called a cab. I wrote a note for Will asking him to pick me up from the clinic when he was done here.

While I waited, I watched Will talking to a small, thick woman with long dark hair. She seemed very upset. I wondered if she was a relative of the hit and run victim? The cab came barreling up.

"Hi." I approached his window. "I have an injured dog I need to get to the vet. Do you think you could help me get her into the cab? I'll pay you extra," I added as I saw his eyebrows shoot up.

Mumbling in a language I didn't understand, the driver helped me lift her and slide her onto the backseat.

We arrived in record time. The driver seemed happy to get us out of the cab. I tipped him extra as promised, and he finally smiled.

Luckily Dr. Messing was there. She had been the one to help me with Karma, a mastiff I befriended last summer, so I trusted her completely to give this dog the best care.

Time dragged as I sat in the waiting room, damp and shivering, my new outfit covered in dog hair. I tried to make the most of my time by reading the pet magazines on the table but my mind kept drifting back to the woman who had died tonight. Did she have kids? A husband? Friends who were going to be devastated by her death? I couldn't even imagine losing one of my friends or sisters like that. I hoped, at least, she didn't feel any pain when it happened. And who could hit someone and just drive away without trying to get them help? One thing was for sure. Will wouldn't rest until the driver was locked up.

"Hey, you." Will hurried through the vet clinic doors and over to my crumpled form molded to the plastic chair. "Sorry, got here as fast as I could."

He held out his hand and helped me out of the chair. "How's the dog?"

I stretched my back and grimaced. "She's sedated and resting."

"That's good. She's going to be okay then?"

"Physically, yeah." I slipped an arm around his waist, under his jacket, as we walked out to his car. "The office manager told me her registered name is Baywater's Silence is Golden, apparently she's a show dog and was microchipped. Her call name is Goldie. She notified the owner, a Victoria Desoto-something—" I glanced up at Will. He had stopped walking. "What's wrong?"

"Victoria Desoto-Roth." His lips tightened. "That means the leash and collar found nearby did belong to her." He glanced down at me and sighed. "The victim of the hit and run. Come on."

My mouth fell open. "So, she was that poor woman's dog? Was she with her when she was hit by the car?"

"Looks like it."

I slid into the seat, trying to fit this information into the puzzle. The blinding light. The impact. Made sense. "So, someone hit this woman and the dog jumped into the water and just swam out to the middle of the bay?"

"Yes."

"Wow. Poor thing. She must have been really traumatized." I suddenly realized what this meant. "Oh no. The clinic will try to call Victoria." But she can't answer. "I wonder if she was married?"

"She had a wedding ring on. That's where I have to go now, to the address on her license and notify the husband." He glanced over at me. "You don't mind waiting in the car while I speak to him, do you?"

"I don't mind." I squeezed his hand. "I didn't know that was part of your job, too."

"Yeah, well, making a death notification is only the half of it. As the investigating detective I have to eliminate the husband as a suspect."

"A suspect? So, you think someone did this on purpose?"

Will shrugged. "There was no sign the driver tried to brake. But, that parking lot is tricky, looks like a road, so the driver could have mistaken it for one. Especially if they were impaired with drugs or alcohol. There was a witness, coming in to dock his boat. He said the driver seemed to be panicking, slipped and fell as she ran to check on the victim. Honestly, I'm thinking a drinking and driving accident. Maybe a tourist who didn't know the area. Or a boat owner. We'll be checking everyone who has a boat docked there."

I pushed up my sleeves, feeling flushed. "So, when the driver saw how bad this Victoria person was injured, they probably took off so they wouldn't go to jail?"

Will shrugged, turning the heater down. "Happens all the time. Witness said the driver seemed to go through the victim's backpack and then tossed it to the side. Maybe looking for an ID. Or money. Who knows?"

I stared out the window. "That woman you were talking to, the one with dark hair, she seemed pretty upset. Was she family?"

"No, that was Jade Harjo, a good friend of the victim. She was actually meeting Mrs. Desoto-Roth there. She said Victoria was excited, that she had an artifact to give her from her uncle's collection after he recently passed. Ms. Harjo apparently helps get Native American artifacts into the museums. They were supposed to meet at Fresco's."

I frowned. "Did Victoria still have the artifact on her?"

"Yeah, we recovered it from her backpack, but it'll be logged as evidence for now so Ms. Harjo will have to wait to claim it."

Will was pulling into the circle drive of a very large stucco house a few miles from where Victoria died. He left the car running and sighed. "Be back."

"Good luck." I watched him make his way to the front door and couldn't help but feel a rush of love and respect for the man. I knew he'd gotten into the business of solving murders because he lost his older brother, Christopher, and no one was ever convicted for it. No family should have to go through that. But, it still took someone with a heart full of compassion to choose this kind of job. I wouldn't want to be the one to tell someone their wife had died, that's for sure.

I turned the heater up as I waited. My clothes were still damp, and I was suddenly very aware I reeked of wet dog. I couldn't wait to get home, take a hot bath and climb under the covers.

About fifteen minutes had gone by before a man emerged from the house, his head down, his gait uncertain, with Will tagging along behind him.

The man was wiping at his nose with a handkerchief as he led Will around to the garage and opened the door. They disappeared inside the garage for just a moment. When they came back out, Will shook the man's hand and gave him a card.

"How'd it go?" I asked as Will slid back into the car, bringing a blast of cool night air in with him.

"He was pretty shaken up. They had an argument this morning, and he said they hadn't spoken before she left. I can't imagine what it would be like to have your spouse leave the house and never return. Especially after a fight."

"Sounds like you don't think he had anything to do with her death? Even though he confessed to them fighting?"

"Nah. He said it was just him being stubborn, nothing big." Will shrugged. "Besides, according to the witness, the car that hit Victoria was a black sedan. The two cars in his garage were a white minivan and a yellow Miata. And the witness said the driver had dark hair pulled back in a ponytail." He smiled. "In case you didn't notice, Eugene Roth barely has enough hair to run a comb through."

Okay, now he was just teasing me. I decided to play along. "But he doesn't have an alibi."

Will chuckled. "This is true."

I held up my index finger dramatically. "And he has motive since he admitted to an argument. Or money is always a motive. That is a pretty big house." Will smirked at me and then moved his eyes back to the road.

"I know, I know," I held up my hands, "leave the detecting to the detectives."

He rested a hand on my knee. "Honestly, Darwin, all kidding aside, I've kind of gotten used to your particular brand of curiosity. I don't mind so much. In fact, your questions keep me thinking outside the box. But, in this case, I don't think there's any big plot to figure out. Just an unfortunate accident. Probably someone out there right now sobering up and quaking in their boots, wondering if they should turn themselves in. We'll still check to see who stood to gain the most from the victim's death, though."

I grinned, feeling warmth spread through me. *Was that acceptance?* "I think that's the nicest thing you've ever said to me."

His blue eyes sparkled as he chuckled. "Well, that's kind of sad. I'll do better."

"You're doing fine." I leaned over and pressed a kiss on his warm cheek. Mmm. He smelled so good. Like a fresh rain. "Oh, did you tell him the good news about their dog? That she survived?"

"Yeah. He said Goldie was Victoria's pride and joy. I told him to contact the emergency clinic."

I nodded. "Good. One problem solved tonight at least. So, what now?"

"Now," Will grinned at me, "we get you home and out of those hair-covered clothes."

CHAPTER FOUR

I had just opened the door to Darwin's Pet Boutique to let in Sylvia's first grooming appointment when my cell phone buzzed in my pocket.

Pulling it out, I frowned then greeted our customer before answering it. "Morning Madeleine." I smiled at the well-dressed woman and her Labradoodle, Micah. "Sylvia will be right with you."

Then, I hurried to answer my phone, since pretty much only my family in Savannah, Frankie and Will called me on it. *Please don't let it be an emergency.* "Hello?"

"Darwin Winters please."

"Speaking." I frowned, not recognizing the voice.

"Hi Darwin, this is Donna at Emergency Veterinary. You brought in an injured golden retriever last night?"

"Oh, yes, how is she?"

"She's doing better. All stitched up. We got her to eat a bite this morning and have her on a light sedative. She's still pretty traumatized."

"Can't blame her." I motioned to Sylvia her client was here. "Did Mr. Roth contact you to pick her up?"

"Yes, that's what I wanted to talk to you about. He called us this morning and asked us to give Goldie back to the breeder."

I stopped in the middle of the aisle. "What? Why?"

"He said Goldie will remind him too much of his wife, and he's not coping well with her death as it is. They have a contract with Baywater Kennel that says Goldie has to go back to them, if for any reason they can no longer care for her."

"Oh." I was still trying to process what she was saying. *The dog has been through hell and now she isn't welcome back in her own home?* My face flushed.

"But, here's the thing. I talked to Linda, the lady who owns the kennel. Dr. Messing put in a good word for you, and so Linda is willing to do a home visit with you so you could adopt her."

Wa.. wa... wait... what?!

She took my silence as her cue to keep talking. "You know, So Goldie doesn't have to go back. After all, she's been through enough, right? She deserves a permanent home."

"Of course she does." I didn't really appreciate the guilt trip being laid on me, but I'd probably do the same thing if I were in her shoes. "She does deserve a home. But..." *Did I really have enough space in my life to give this traumatized dog the attention she deserved?* I pinched the bridge of my nose and counted to ten. *It would be nice to have a dog around again.* "Okay. So, say I agree to adopt her, what's the next step?"

"Oh, yes, great question." I heard the relief in her voice. "Well, you can pick her up any time this afternoon. I'll give Linda your contact information, and she'll call you to set up the home visit. Shouldn't be any trouble at all. I just know you and Goldie will be a great match."

"Thanks. All right, I guess I'll see you this afternoon." I hung up. I supposed I was picking up the bill, too. Not that money was the issue. Abandoning a pet was.

I rang up a few early morning customers and then snuck back to talk to Sylvia. Leaning against the glass window that separated her grooming room from the main part of the boutique, I crossed my arms and watched her expertly trim Micah's nails as she spoke soothing Portuguese to him.

"Remember the golden retriever we found and took to the vet last night?"

Sylvia flicked a silky dark bang out of her eye, glancing at me. "*Si?*"

"When Charlie comes in this afternoon, I'm going to go pick her up. I'll be taking care of her for a bit." I wasn't ready to say I'd be keeping her. There was a chance the home visit wouldn't turn out great. What if this Linda person thought I worked too much? Or wouldn't have enough time to exercise her? There could be any number of reasons she'd take her back. Goldie was a show dog. What if she wanted to keep her and show her?

Sylvia's brow shot up. "Because?"

"Her owner apparently can't. Reminds him too much of his late wife. So, she needs a place to go right now."

"*Aí não*, that is no good." Sylvia shook her head, flashing me a smile. "You were the child who brought home stray kittens, no?"

Kittens. Birds. Frogs. And once a litter of naked, pink, orphaned baby moles.

I sighed. "That would be me. What could I say though? She's already had her world torn apart. And a posh world it was, apparently. She was a show dog."

"Well." She shrugged and patted the champagne-colored Labradoodle on his rump. "Now she will be a pet boutique dog. Not so bad a life."

I smiled. I loved Sylvia's optimism. "Not a bad life at all." *Unless I could find her a better home. Maybe she could still be a show dog for someone.*

The steady flow of pet-loving snowbirds kept me busy enough that I didn't have time to think about Goldie again until Charlie came in at one o'clock. Charlie Nichols was a vet tech student at St. Pete College who we hired in December to make sure we could take a lunch break during tourist season. Especially after my sister, Mallory, went back home.

We had to work around Charlie's classes but she was great with the customers. If I had to describe Charlie in two words it would be dependable and colorful. She had pink hair, tattoo "sleeves", a silver stud in her left nostril and a heart bigger than the state of Texas. Her passion for helping animals was the thing that shone through and got her hired. It didn't hurt that she believed in the supernatural. I learned that from her interest in the flower essence.

"Hey, Charlie." I greeted her as she shoved her bag under the counter. "How'd the anatomy test go?"

"Aced it." She held up her hand, and I gave her a high five.

"Good for you. I'd feel bad if working here was taking away from your study time." Not that she needed it. The more I got to know Charlie, the more I realized what a brilliant mind sat under those strange hats she was so fond of. I handed a regular customer her bag of homemade dog treats. She came in just about every day now to buy them with her chubby gray terrier.

"No worries." Turning back to me, Charlie adjusted her skull cap. Pink streaked hair stuck out around the edges. "Besides, a girl's gotta eat. I'd be living on ramen noodles if you guys hadn't hired me. Speakin' of... you need to go get some lunch. Go." She bumped me playfully with her hip. "I got it from here."

"All right. But, I'll be bringing back more than lunch today." I sighed as I grabbed my straw bag and sweater from under the counter. "Darwin's Pet Boutique is going to have a new mascot." Her eyebrow rose. "Long story," I added. Then I patted her arm and headed out to grab a taxi.

CHAPTER FIVE

Right before closing time, Frankie popped in the boutique with Itty and Bitty, her two Chihuahuas. Frankie's a former homeless lady who won the lottery and she's also one of my best friends here in St. Pete.

Charlie was ringing up Sarah Applebaum, our last customer.

"Hey, Sarah and Charlie. Got some dessert here you gals are welcomed to," Frankie called.

"Thanks but no thanks. Trying to watch my figure." Sarah patted her plump hips. "Divorce is almost final, and I plan on jumping in the dating pool."

"I hear ya." Frankie dropped the box of goodies on the tea table by the window. "It's slim pickings out there, let me tell you. Just a bunch of crabs with too much baggage." Then she frowned at me. "You look tired, sugarplum. Rough day? Oh!" She spotted Goldie lying under the table, tongue hanging out, eyes searching the passersby relentlessly. "Hello. Who's this?"

I sighed. "This is Goldie. Long story short, Will and I were on the pirate ship for Mike's wedding Saturday night and we fished her out of the ocean.

Poor thing's owner was hit by a car and killed while walking her down by the pier—"

"Shoot!" Frankie smacked the table. "I read about that in the paper. Victoria Desoto-Roth. I met her once at a fund raiser. So sad, she was a nice lady."

"Oh, Victoria?" Sarah shook her head as she loaded up her arms with her bagged purchases. "She was a real sweetheart. So tragic. This is her dog?"

"Yep. I'm keeping her for awhile. Maybe finding her a home so she can show again."

"But, Victoria was married," Frankie said. "What about her husband? Doesn't he want her?"

"No. He said Goldie just reminds him too much of his wife, and he's apparently devastated and can't handle seeing her. He wanted her given back to the kennel."

Frankie's hand went to her hip. "Well, that's just crap. How does he think Goldie feels? Losing her mom and now her home?" Frankie shook her head. "Would he give up a child, too, if they had one?" She bent down and gave each of her dogs a treat from the bowl on the table. I noticed they were getting a bit plump. "Makes me so mad."

"Don't even get me started." I opened the box she'd brought. The scent of cinnamon filled the boutique. "Cinnamon buns. You're killing me, Frankie." I expected Sylvia to appear as soon as the scent reached the back where she was cleaning up her grooming room. I pulled a sticky bun from the box and shook my head. "I guess we really shouldn't judge him. We have no idea what he can and can't handle emotionally. I mean, the man's wife just got killed. I don't think any of us know how we'd react or what we could handle."

"I suppose you're right." Frankie grabbed a cup and poured hot water over a tea infuser filled with a new peach white tea. "This stuff smells heavenly." She took a big whiff of her cup and sighed. "I guess I've just been around too many people who lost everything and were still strong because they had to be. There was no other option."

I knew she was thinking about the people she used to live with at Pirate City, the homeless camp. I'm sure she's seen more than her fair share of tragedy.

"Well, good on you for taking care of her dog, Darwin," Sarah said. "Poor thing. All right, I gotta get Lady Elizabeth's food home before she starts gnawing on my couch pillows again."

I went and opened the door for her. "Have a great evening, Sarah. Give Lady Elizabeth a kiss from us."

"Will do. Bye, ladies."

I locked the door behind her then leaned against it and kicked off the lovely suede heels Sylvia had bought me for Christmas. Looking down at my red, swollen toes, I decided I was going back to wearing flip flops. Fashion just wasn't worth it. I'd leave that to Sylvia.

I grabbed a water bottle from under the counter and crawled under the table to pour some in the bowl I had placed next to Goldie. Then I stroked her gently around her shaved fur and checked her stitches. She whined and sniffed the water but didn't drink it.

"She's been lying here all day looking out the window. I think she's looking for Victoria. How sad is that?"

"Pretty damn sad," Frankie said.

"Poor thing." Charlie straightened a stack of our new harness lined t-shirts. "So... did you get any info from Will? You know, about Victoria's death? Like did they find the hit and run driver?"

"No, they're still investigating. Witnesses said it was a lady in a black sedan and she got out and went over to check Victoria, went through her backpack and then took off. That's all we know so far."

"She didn't even call 911?" Frankie asked.

"Nope. A guy docking his boat did." I shrugged. "And Will said there were no brake marks. So..."

"Someone hit her on purpose?" Charlie froze. "Like murdered her?"

"I don't know if I'd call it murder," I said, making some peach tea for myself. "Will seems to think it was something less premeditated. Like they were drunk and didn't want to get caught by calling the police."

I could hear Sylvia's heels clicking on the wood floor as she came toward the front of the boutique. I smiled to myself.

"Are those cinnamon buns that smell so heavenly?"

"Yeah, you want to split one with me?" I teased.

Her dark eyes sparkled. "*Hola*? Do you know me?" She laughed, digging a fat, gooey one out of the box and moaning as she took a bite.

Frankie chuckled. "A girl after my own heart."

"How's our new pup doing?" Sylvia asked after swallowing and peering under the table.

"Still the same." I sipped my tea. "The flower essence isn't helping yet." I may have to resort to some magick before the poor thing stresses herself into a stroke.

By the time we finished chatting and locked up, it was past eight o'clock. The shops were closed but Beach Drive was hopping with restaurant-goers. Luckily, I lived in the townhouse right above our pet boutique, so I didn't have far to walk Goldie. Poor thing slunk down, glued to my leg, her eyes searching every face that passed us.

"It's okay, Goldie. That's it," I cooed to her as I led her to the entrance. By the time we entered the townhouse, she was trembling again. I threw my bag, shoes and keys on the counter. She crouched down right inside the doorway and refused to budge, so I let her stay there and get adjusted to the place while I went to make her some food.

"This will be your new home for a while, girl." I talked softly to her while I opened the can of prescription food Dr. Messing had recommended. "I know you're sad and confused, but I will do everything I can to make you feel better." I dug under the sink for the metal bowl I used for Karma when he lived here. Touching it brought back a flood of memories of him. I smiled. In the last photo his new family had emailed me, he was fat and happy with a big old goofy grin. Mad Dog would be happy to know what a good life he had now. I sighed. Still missed him, though. Such a gentle soul.

"Okay, Goldie." I plopped the food into the bowl and added some kibble to it. "You've got to eat." I walked around to the front of the counter and placed it on the floor. Goldie dropped her head on the floor between her paws and stared up at me with the most haunted brown eyes I've ever seen on a creature. And then she spoke, an almost imperceptible whine. My heart tugged in my chest like someone had a string attached to it. I fell to the floor in front of her.

"Oh, baby." I reached out and stroked a long, silky ear, tears suddenly pooling in my eyes. I blinked them back. "I can tell you and your mom loved each other very much, and I know you miss her. But, she would want you to eat, to survive." I lay down beside her and draped an arm over her. She might not be able to understand my words, but she could read my body language. I had to get her to trust me so we could work on her healing. I snuggled my face into her neck. "I'll stay right here with you until you're ready. I'm not leaving you."

I awoke to darkness. My arm was asleep and I was freezing. What the...? I glanced around. Why was I lying on the floor by the front door? A scraping sound caught my attention. I craned my stiff neck to see the outline of a dog with its head in the metal bowl. Oh yeah. Goldie.

"Good girl."

I pushed myself off the floor with the arm that wasn't tingling like crazy and padded into the kitchen to get her some water. I added a few drops of honeysuckle and fringed violet flower essence, my recipe for grief, and quietly placed the bowl on the floor next to the one she was now licking clean.

"That's a good girl, Goldie." I stroked her side, being mindful of her stitches, while she lapped at the water. "Your mom would be very proud of you." I glanced at the clock. One in the morning. "Okay, girl, let's get a few hours of sleep. Come on." I led her up the stairs and patted the bed. She hopped up and turned in a circle, finally settling down and looking at me with those sad eyes.

I changed into an oversized t-shirt and crawled under the crisp, cool covers beside her, snuggling up next to her warm body. Every once in awhile, I felt her body tremble.

"I wish you could give me more to go on." Victoria deserved to have some closure, some justice, and so did this poor creature now sharing my bed. I squeezed my eyes shut. *No. Will was investigating. He had it covered and you promised him you'd try to stay out of trouble. Just go to sleep, Darwin.*

CHAPTER SIX

"Come on lazy bones, you can't lie in bed all day." I had already meditated, showered and dressed, and Goldie hadn't moved from her curled up position on the bed. At least the shaking had stopped, that was something. "Well, I'm going downstairs and make us some breakfast. You come down when you're ready."

I was out on the balcony checking on the flowers when a nose nudged the French door open wider and Goldie looked up at me.

"Well, good morning, Miss Sunshine. Glad you decided to join me." I removed my cheesecloth glove and walked over to her. Kneeling down, I took her snout in my hands. "I don't think I've ever seen a sad golden retriever before." Her ears even drooped. I touched my nose to hers. Cool and wet. That was a good sign.

"What am I going to do with you?" I mean, when I had to help Karma out of his funk that was one thing. Mastiffs always look sad and worried. Goldens though? They were the happy-go-lucky children of the dog world, with their beaming perma-smile and soul sparkle. "Come on; let's see if you touched your breakfast." I kissed her between her watery eyes and led her back to the kitchen. The food was half gone from her bowl. Another good sign. Feeling encouraged, I got ready for the day ahead.

At the boutique, Goldie stuffed herself beneath the table once again, her nose pressed against the window. Looking for Victoria, no doubt. Broke my heart but at least the desperate panting had stopped.

Frankie and her pups came in around lunchtime after Charlie arrived. I was ready for a break.

"How's Goldie doing today?" She peered under the table before taking a seat and helping herself to tea. Itty and Bitty sniffed Goldie's backside with their tiny little noses and then sat down for their treats.

"She did eat some this morning." I plopped down in the chair across from her and fixed my own tea. "But I think she's still watching for her momma to come get her."

"I'm sure it'll just take her time. Time heals all they say." Frankie flipped open the morning paper. "Of course, a good massage helps, too."

I didn't watch the news so Frankie's morning paper commentary was my only source of information about the world outside my little bubble. "Do they have dog masseuses?" I asked. *That might be a good thing to bring to our boutique once a month. A dog masseuse.*

"Masseuses, acupuncturists, spas, you name it," a customer in line chimed in. "Pet pampering is a big business."

"Interesting. Well, Goldie here was a show dog, so she probably got the royal treatment," I said.

Frankie refolded the paper. "Speaking of, says there's a dog show on Saturday at Azalea Park."

"I used to show bichons," a petite woman with short curly hair offered. "But, the atmosphere in the show world is too cutthroat. Just lost its appeal for me."

"Yeah, I've heard how competitive those folks get." Frankie took off her reading glasses. "Remember that really pretty white dog a little while back that died from rat poisoning a few days after competing at Westminster? So tragic."

I stared at her in horror. "Someone poisoned a dog because of a dog show?"

"Westminster isn't just any dog show."

"Still!" I rubbed my arms for comfort.

Frankie nodded. "You never know what people are capable of."

Just then a customer was entering and held the door open wide for Jeanie as she was leaving. Goldie suddenly scooted backwards from beneath the table and scrambled to the door, bolting through it before poor Jeanie could get out a gasp.

"Goldie!" I cried, jumping off the chair and running through the door after her. *Where did she go?* I scanned the sidewalk to the left, then right. Crowds were already milling about, too thick to spot her. I ran across the street, between stopped traffic and into North Straub Park. Turning circles, panic and frustration tied my insides up in knots. *How could a dog disappear so quickly? What if she gets hit by a car?* She was still operating in anxiety mode so she wouldn't be acting like a normal dog.

Frankie was waving to me across the street. Defeated, I made my way back over to her.

"Hey, sugar, I know you can't leave the boutique right now, so I'll drive around and look for her. She couldn't have gotten far."

"Okay. Thanks, Frankie." I gave the area one more scan.

"I'm so sorry, Darwin," a devastated Jeanie said as I came back into the boutique.

I gave her a quick reassuring hug. "It's all right. You go on. I'm sure we'll find her."

Frankie kept me updated by text which areas she was searching. I was trying not to think about what would happen if Linda decided to call me for a home visit before I had found Goldie. *Oh yeah, sure. We'll let you adopt a prize-winning golden retriever you've already let run away to god-knows-where. Not.*

Two hours had crawled by without luck when my phone vibrated with a number I didn't recognize. "Hello?"

"Is this Darwin Winters?"

"Yes?"

"My name is Eugene Roth. Linda over at Baywater Kennel gave me your number. I... um... she told me you had picked up Goldie and well, she's here. I just got home and found her on the front porch. Can you come get her?"

I had stopped in the middle of typing a customer's phone number into the computer. So many thoughts and emotions were assaulting me I couldn't get a handle on a single one.

"Miss Winters?"

She had gone home? My heart dropped like a rock into my stomach. Poor, grieving soul. I squeezed the collar I was ringing up and closed my eyes. "I'm here. Yes. I'll come get her after I close my pet boutique. I know where you live." I hung up and stared at my palm. The diamond pattern from the collar's hardware was stamped onto it. Tears filled my eyes. "Unbelievable."

"Everything all right?" Mr. Keller asked, his ancient, yellowed eyes peering at me with compassion under unruly white brows.

I swiped at my eyes with the back of my hand. "Sure. Yeah. Fine." I really had to concentrate hard to finish the transaction. "I just wonder how some people can walk around without a heart. Thought that was kind of a requirement for being a human being."

Mr. Keller smiled knowingly. "Known plenty of heartless humans in my time. I'm sure there's a special place in hell for 'em." He chuckled.

I gave him a thankful smile as I handed him his purchase. "Well, you're definitely not one of them, Mr. Keller. You have yourself a great day, now."

CHAPTER SEVEN

It wasn't difficult to find Eugene's house again. As the cab pulled up, I thought about the night Victoria died and how I had sat in the driveway while Will notified Eugene that his wife wouldn't be coming home. My skin warmed at the thought of Will. He acted so tough sometimes, but the man had secret stores of compassion it was a real privilege to witness.

"Can you wait here, please?" I scooted out of the back of the cab. "I should only be a minute."

I hurried to the front porch of the two-story, yellow stucco place and rang the bell. Eugene answered the door. I had only viewed him from a distance before. Close up, he looked like a wreck. His eyes were puffy and his pupils were dilated like maybe he was on something. His already pale German features were positively ghostly. All my visions of giving him a piece of my mind faded away. No need to beat a man when he's this down. As he motioned for me to come in, I stepped into the foyer and offered him a small smile of sympathy instead.

"I'm so sorry for the loss of your wife, Mr. Roth. I can't imagine how devastated you must be."

"Thanks. You have no idea." He choked and then closed his eyes to compose himself. "Goldie is upstairs under the bed." He motioned for me to follow him to the grand stairway. His gait was still impeded, like he was moving in slow motion. Probably still in shock. Okay, maybe Goldie was better off somewhere else. He clearly was barely taking care of himself. "It's where she used to hide from thunderstorms and fireworks. I tried all of her favorite treats. Nothing will coax her out."

He led me upstairs and then down a hall to a cavernous master bedroom. A king-sized brass bed, covered in a gold silk comforter and piles of large pillows, ate up a good chunk of space, but there was still room for two large dressers and a wardrobe closet. Matching gold silk curtains hung on the windows. I removed my flip flops before stepping from the Mexican tile onto the plush cream carpeting. I detected the same scent of lilacs that I had received from Goldie, only it was faded here. *So, it was Victoria's perfume Goldie smelled and not a clue to the killer? Good to know.*

A black and white framed photo of Goldie and a smiling woman sat on the nightstand. I picked it up. "Your wife?"

"Yes."

"She was real pretty." My heart squeezed with sadness. Okay, let's get this over with. "Goldie, sweetie?" I called, kneeling down to peer under the bed. Yep, she was there. No heavy panting, just sad eyes uninterested in me being there. No tail wag. No movement. "Oh, girl." I sighed. She obviously wasn't going to come out on her own, and I wasn't about to drag her out. This was going to take some time and maybe even some magick.

I glanced up at Eugene, leaning against the doorframe like the wall was holding him upright. "Mr. Roth, I think this is going to take some time to get her out. Would you mind telling the cab driver he can go? I'll just call another one when we get her out."

He nodded, seemingly relieved to have something to do. "Of course. I'll just leave you to it. I'll be in my office downstairs then. Good luck." He moved away, and I collapsed onto the carpet, staring at Goldie. I slipped my arm slowly under the bed and held one of her paws. She didn't jerk it away, which was good. Of course, it could be she just didn't care. That was bad.

I lay there for a few minutes, just holding her paw, whispering to her. No change. All right, time for a little help.

Rising and padding across the room, I flipped on the light switch to the attached bathroom and glanced around. A spa that could have held ten people or one small elephant dominated the room. Gold fixtures gleamed from it and the double sinks set in the marble countertop. White fur rugs kept bare feet protected from the cold tile. Kneeling down, I opened the cabinet under one of the sinks. I needed a container. Weaved baskets held bucket loads of creams, foundations, eye-shadows, lipstick and various other types of make-up. Good grief, Victoria must have loved her cosmetics. I moved to the second cabinet.

Three-tier glass shelves had been placed inside. On the shelves sat a collection of nail polish and stick-on nails that would have rivaled a store. Another basket held packages of silk pantyhose and sheer stockings. I felt my face grow hot. There had to be something inappropriate about viewing a deceased woman's private things. I was about to close the cabinet when behind the basket, a jar of hair-ties caught my eye. I pulled it out. Glass. Perfect. I dumped the hair-ties out onto the counter and filled the jar with water. It wasn't my chalice, tuned to my personal vibration, but it would do.

I carried the jar back to the bedroom and sat cross-legged on the carpet with it in my lap. Closing my eyes, I began to breathe deeply, following my breath in and out of my body until I felt myself seated in the center of my being. From here, I could reach out to the water, my own energy like an arm extending into the water molecules, exciting them, changing them. Water had magical properties all its own and since living beings were mostly water, it was a great healing tool.

I concentrated on infusing feelings of love and well-being into the water molecules. This hadn't ever been one of my strongest talents, and I was a bit rusty. I could almost feel Grandma Winter's disappointment in me. I shook it off. Let it go. I began to feel my concentration waver. I forced it back to the task at hand. Time ticked by, but I had no idea how much.

I blinked as the lilac smell of the room and the solidness of the floor beneath me returned. Darn. I wasn't finished, but I was drained so this would have to be good enough.

Scooting down on my belly, I slid under the bed, being careful not to spill the water.

"Hey there, Goldie," I whispered. She moved her eyes to me but didn't lift her muzzle from the carpet. "I need you to drink this for me. It'll make you feel better." I hoped.

I dipped a finger in the water and held it in front of her nose. Her nostrils flared as she sniffed it. I waited. If she didn't take it, I could resort to rubbing it on her gums, but she wouldn't get enough that way. Not as weak as this water was. "Come on, sweetie. You can do it." Goldie's tongue slid out, and I felt the warm sandpaper-like sensation as she licked my finger. "Good girl." I moved the jar in front of her and tilted it so the water sat at the edge of the lip. "Good girl. Have a drink. Go on." She dipped her tongue in the jar and then began lapping at the water. I felt the knots in my body relax. "That's a girl, Goldie. I knew you were a fighter."

I stroked her fur and hummed as I waited for the water to take effect. I had rested my head on my hand and was feeling exhaustion tug at me when Goldie began to stir. She lifted her head and then placed a paw on my arm. Definitely the highlight of my day.

"Well, hello. There you are, girl." I smiled into her eyes. They didn't quite sparkle but she was at least present now and watching me. "What do you say we get out of here?" I began to scoot back. "Come on." I paused when only my head remained under the bed. "Good girl," I whispered. "Come on, it's time to go. Your mom isn't coming back here. I'm sorry." Her ears twitched and she stretched out a paw to me, then the other one. As I encouraged her, she scooted on her belly until she emerged from the bed. Standing, she shook her whole body and stared at me, ears down. I kneeled and wrapped my arms around her, letting her rest her head on my shoulder. "Okay." I nodded, swiping at a stray tear. "Let's go home." Dumping the water into the sink, I replaced the hair-ties and the jar.

"Mr. Roth?" I called after descending the stairs. Goldie stood beside me, glued to my leg.

Eugene emerged from a room somewhere to the left. "Oh, you got her out, I see."

"Yes." I rested a hand protectively on her head. "I've called a cab."

"Right." He glanced at Goldie. "She seems to like you. I'm glad. Victoria—" he choked on her name and cleared his throat. "She is... was really important to my wife. She would be happy to know Goldie is in good hands." He sniffed and held out a hand. "Please, make yourself comfortable in the living room while you wait."

I followed him around to a sunken living area with overstuffed leather couches.

"Can I get you anything to drink?"

"No, thank you." I sat down and Goldie sat with me, leaning hard against my leg.

"Oh, I almost forgot, I have a bag for you. Goldie's toothbrush, favorite toys and other things. Be right back."

I was drained. Resting my chin on the hand that wasn't stroking Goldie, I scanned the magazines on the coffee table. It was funny how much you could tell about a person from what they chose to read. Eugene hadn't gotten rid of Victoria's magazines obviously. That must be the hardest thing to do when a loved one is gone... throw out the personal things that belonged to them, that could remind you of them. There was The Canine Chronicle, Dog Fancy, The Retriever Journal. "You definitely were the center of your mom's world," I whispered, scratching under Goldie's ear. There was also a Vogue, a Victoria Secrets Catalog, a Forbes and Smart Money. Beneath the Smart Money there was a notebook sticking out, the handwriting on the top said: Biggest CD faux pas? CD on a budget? *Maybe Eugene's an accountant or investment banker? Yeah, that seems to fit him.*

There was a honk outside.

"That'd be for us, girl, come on."

Eugene met us at the door with the bag of Goldie's belongings. He handed Goldie a stuffed alligator, which she took gently from him, her tail swishing a few times. His lip quivered. "That's Gator. Her favorite." Then he nodded. "Thank you, Miss Winters. My wife, she would be very grateful to you."

I felt a wave of heavy emotion wash over me as he shook my hand. I wanted to tell him he could visit Goldie at any time, but I knew he wouldn't take me up on the offer.

"You take care now," I said instead.

That night I tossed and turned, awoke in a sweat more than once after dreams of getting hit by a car. *Or were they memories?* I lay in the dark with my arm draped across Goldie, stroking her belly, unable to shake the images of the headlights or the feeling something was very wrong. As my hand brushed the shaved area of Goldie's body, I suddenly remembered our conversation in the boutique about the cutthroat world of dog shows. *What if the person did hit them on purpose? And what if they weren't trying to hurt Victoria... but Goldie?*

CHAPTER EIGHT

Two women approached the counter the next morning. One carried a plump, shivering Chihuahua mix.

I smiled. "Hi, ladies, did you find everything all right?"

"Yes," the one holding the dog said. "And I was told you do birthday cakes for dogs? Do you have a catalog or something?"

"Sure do." I pulled the photo album from beneath the counter and handed it to her. "These are the standard cakes I've made, but if you had something in mind you don't see here, just ask."

She passed the dog off to her friend to flip through the book.

I didn't reach out and touch the shaking dog. I was feeling vulnerable and didn't need to expose myself to this little guy's angst. "What's your cutie's name?" I asked instead.

The woman held up his paw and waved it. He pulled his upper lip back in what I hoped was a smile. "This is Bandit. He's a real drama queen."

"Well, that's a perfect name for you." I chuckled at the dog as he snuck a lick at the woman's cheek. He had a black mask that did indeed make him look like a bandit.

"Oh, what do you think about this one, Bernice? It's a fire hydrant," Bandit's owner said.

"I think Bandit wouldn't know whether to eat it or pee on it."

She waved her friend off. "Well, I think it's perfect. I'll take that one."

"It is a favorite." I smiled as I found her an order form and pointed at the table by the window. "You can have a seat while you fill this out. Grab yourself a cup of tea and there's some human cookies over there, too."

"Go on, I've got Bandit," Bernice said, riffling through some of the items in the baskets with her free hand.

I moved out of the way as Charlie led an elderly woman up to the counter to ring up her purchases.

Charlie pushed a pink-streaked chunk of hair out of her eye. "Hey, Darwin, Mrs. Tilley's cat is recovering from surgery. We have something to help her with that, yes?"

"Sure do. Be right back." I grabbed a bottle of flower essence from the back, wrapped it in tissue paper and tucked it into Mrs. Tilley's bag. "No charge on that, Charlie," I whispered. "Now, Mrs. Tilley, just put a few drops on her throughout the day or you can put them in her water."

Mrs. Tilley's grin puffed up her cheeks which pushed up her glasses. "Thank you, dear."

I nodded as Bandit's owner approached the counter with the cake order form. "All done?"

"Yes." She handed me the order form. "I'll go ahead and pay for that now."

I waited until Charlie was done to enter her information into the computer. I read her delivery address. I wasn't familiar with that area.

"Twentieth Street? Which part of town is that?" I asked. If I wasn't familiar with it, I probably wouldn't be able to bike there. I'd have to take a taxi.

"Oh I live across from the Pinellas Point Indian Mound. Bernice here is my neighbor."

"Oh, okay. I haven't visited that place yet."

Bernice shook her head. "Yeah, well. Now's probably not the time to go. Some crazy has been digging up the Mound lately. The neighborhood started doing nightly patrols to curb the vandalism. We've put a lot of effort in through the years to stop the erosion, planting native plants and getting the fence put up. But we'll have to stop the patrols now. Our neighbor's husband got attacked there last night and is in the hospital with a concussion. It's getting too dangerous."

My hand poised over the mouse, I stared at Bernice. "What in heaven's name happened?"

"Don't know. He just said someone hit him in the head from behind when he went to check on a noise. He was surprised but managed to grab their legs and got in a bit of a scuffle. It ended when he said the guy hit him in the head again with a shovel."

Bandit's owner cleared her throat and leaned closer to us. "His wife told me he thought it was actually a woman. But, he's too embarrassed to tell the police that he got knocked out by a woman."

I stared at her, thinking about the woman who killed Victoria. Could it be the same person? Surely, that would be too much of a coincidence. On the other hand, how many psychotic women are running around St. Pete right now? "That's kind of important information for him to keep to himself," I said.

"I know." She nodded, stroking Bandit's head. "But, he's already insecure about being short. If he did get knocked out by a woman, he'll take that to his grave."

If it was the same woman who killed Victoria, why would she be digging up the Mound? Victoria was delivering an artifact to Jade. Could an artifact have something to do with the attack at the Mound, too?

I tore off the pink customer copy of her order and handed it to her. "Do you think someone is digging illegally for artifacts there? Maybe to sell? Money is always a viable motive for violence."

She shrugged. "I don't think there's anything of value buried there. I know they've found some shell tools, stuff like that. But, if someone were digging up artifacts illegally, wouldn't be too hard to find a buyer. I've heard rumors about the guy who owns Treasure Coast Artifacts, Barnie something. People say he'll buy anything and has even been arrested for poaching artifacts himself."

"Maybe they're not trying to dig something up," Bernice lowered her voice with a touch of humor. "Maybe they are trying to bury something... or someone. After all, it is a burial Mound."

Her friend shot her an amused look. "What? In pieces?"

They shared a laugh as they waved and Bernice held the door open for a customer to enter.

I stared after them, their words stirring something inside me that was making me nauseous. Shaking my head, I forced a smile when the customer, a middle-aged woman with her long blonde ponytail sticking through a baseball cap, approached me.

"Hi, can I help you with something today?"

"Yes, I'm looking for Darwin Winters." Despite the baseball cap and jeans, she had a business-like air about her.

"I'm Darwin."

"Oh good." She glanced around the boutique and then offered me her hand. "I'm Linda from Baywater Kennel. I was in the neighborhood and thought we could get the home visit for Goldie's adoption out of the way."

"Oh!" My heart did a funky little beat against my chest. "Of course. She's usually by my side here all day, but I let her sleep in this morning. She was really restless last night." *So, I gave her some love and peace-infused water this morning but no need to mention that.* "I was planning on going up to fetch her soon." *Heavens, why did she have to come the one time I left Goldie alone?* I rubbed the back of my neck where beads of sweat had broken out under my hairline. "Let me just go see if my partner can watch the boutique for a few minutes while we run up. I live above the boutique."

* * *

"Goldie," I called as we entered the townhouse. "Here, girl."

"This is a very nice place. Plenty of room for a dog." Linda walked to the French doors and peered out.

There was a thump upstairs. "She must still be in bed." I laughed nervously. "Come on up."

The sight that greeted us left me speechless. I could only stare at Goldie, who trotted out of the bathroom, her tail wagging, her face covered in baby powder and one of my bras stuck around her neck by the arm strap. There was also a trail of toilet paper around the room, over the bed and shredded magazines littering the carpet.

I lifted my hands and covered my face, stealing a glance at Linda. Her mouth had dropped open as she took in the damage. Goldie came over and sat in front of us, her dark eyes shining, her tail swooshing, making the magazine bits beneath her tumble across the carpet.

She let out a sharp bark and we both jumped.

"Oh, girl." I kneeled down and gently removed my bra from around Goldie's neck. My humiliation was complete. "I don't know what got into her," I stuttered. *Was this a reaction to the magick-infused water?* "She hasn't done anything like this before." I picked up some of the toilet paper and tried to wipe off the baby powder from her eyes and snout. She sneezed a few times and then play bowed. I couldn't help it. I started to laugh. Hysterically. Like, holding my stomach, tears flowing down my face, trying to catch my breath kind of laughter. Goldie seemed pleased with her redecorating skills and my reaction. She pounced on me and licked the tears from my face with vigor.

"I'm... so... sorry," I tried to get out between snorts and giggles and licks. "I know this looks really bad." I tilted my head back and looked up at Linda, ready to throw myself at her mercy. *At this moment, I knew I really wanted this. I really wanted this sweet creature in my life.*

But there was no need to worry. Linda was smiling and shaking her head. "Actually, this is perfect. Rarely does an opportunity come up in a home visit where I can see how a person would react to the dog being mischievous. I can see you really care about Goldie, and you two already have a special bond. I have to say, I'm very surprised that she's so happy considering the trauma she's just been through."

My heart soared and I jumped up and took her by surprise with a hug. "Thank you. Does this mean you're approving the adoption?"

Linda reached down and scratched Goldie behind the ear, sending a puff of baby powder into the air. "Yes, I believe you'll give her the home and love she needs." She grinned. "But first, I suggest you give her a bath."

* * *

I locked the boutique door and turned the closed sign around. Heavens, it had been a long, emotional day. A knock on the glass startled me. I turned around to see a young, dark-haired woman waving. I glanced longingly at the tea before unlocking the door.

"I'm so sorry. We're closed up for the day." I hoped my tired cheeks formed a smile instead of a grimace.

Her face was tan and her eyes were glassy. "I know. I don't mean to bother you. My name is Josie Desoto... Victoria was my cousin. Eugene told me you adopted Goldie, and I was just wondering if I could see her?"

"Oh." I opened the door wider. "Sure. I'm sure she'd be happy to see a familiar face." I led her over to where Goldie was stretched out on her pillow behind the counter, her fur shining and smelling good from the bath Sylvia had given her. "I'm so sorry for your loss."

"Thanks. Hey there, sweet thing." Josie dropped to her knees, despite a tight leather skirt and sky high boots, and took Goldie's head in her hands. Goldie's tail flicked the floor and she licked Josie's hand. "Oh, you poor baby." She pressed a kiss between Goldie's eyes and rubbed her ears. "Goldie and Victoria were inseparable." She shook her head. "She looks good. Real good. You're a doll for taking care of her."

"I actually just got approval today to adopt her. She's a sweetheart. I was kind of shocked Eugene didn't want to keep her, until I saw him yesterday. I guess he's having a hard enough time taking care of himself."

She rolled her eyes. "Yeah, he's not a real stable person, anyway. Goldie's better off here. He barely paid attention to Victoria, always holed up in that office writing. He'd probably forget to feed her." She ran her hand next to the shaved fur and examined the stitches. "That's gonna leave a scar. Looks like it's healing nicely though." She shook her head. "Glad Victoria can't see this. I think this scar would disqualify her from showing. She wanted Goldie here to be the first golden retriever to win the Westminster Dog Show. That's all she talked about."

Westminster? That's where Frankie said that white dog was poisoned. So, Victoria was shooting for the big win? Bigger stakes, more to lose. That makes it all the more plausible a rival would want Goldie out of the competition.

Just then Charlie came out of the back. Josie stood up as I introduced her to Charlie as Victoria's cousin.

"Nice to meet you. Like your tattoo. Looks fresh," Charlie said, admiring her forearm.

Josie twisted her arm, giving us a better view. It was a black and white sword, a skull with an eye patch and pirate hat overlaid on it and a ribbon with the word: Eternity. It did look red. "Yeah, just got this one." She adjusted her large bag on the other shoulder. "Have a few I wish I didn't but this one has meaning. It's in memory of my dad. Even if he could be a jerk, he was still my dad."

Charlie nodded and grew serious. "So sorry about your cousin. Were you two very close?"

"We were getting there. We've had our family issues plus... I've lived in Vegas for almost seven years now so we didn't see each other much anymore. I spent some time here last summer and we hung out. She was a good person, though. I always looked up to her. She took good care of my dad. We lost him recently, too. That's why I came here, for his funeral."

Well, good grief. She lost her dad and her cousin? How awful.

"I didn't realize you had lost your dad so recently, Josie. Let me fix you some hot tea." It was the only comfort I could think to give.

She planted one more kiss on Goldie's snout and then followed me over to the table. "I'm not sure what to do." She sighed. "I probably should just sell dad's house and stay in Vegas. It's where I'm me. If that makes sense." I nodded. She took the cup I offered her. "Thanks. Plus, God knows I need the money." Then she pulled a flask out of her bag and poured a generous dollop of something that smelled like whiskey into the tea. I pressed my lips together to keep my mouth from falling open. She took a swig and closed her eyes. "Mmm. That's good. Thanks."

"It's raspberry." After I spoke, I realized she probably couldn't taste the tea anyway. I glanced over at Charlie, who was straightening out a display shelf nearby and biting her lip, which meant she was trying not to laugh.

"Course, getting a fresh start in a new place would be good, too," Josie continued, glancing out the window. "Life gets so... complicated when you're in one place too long."

I sipped my tea, nodding. I had no idea what she was talking about but it seemed like she needed someone to talk to, so I listened.

"Now that dad's house is mine, I could stay. If he doesn't haunt me." She broke out into something like a laugh and then sniffed. "He didn't leave it to me, you know. The house?" She looked at me with one brow raised. "Isn't that something? He left it to Victoria, instead of his own daughter. But, jokes on him now cause it's mine anyways." She laughed again, but in a way that was painful to hear.

I blinked in surprise. *Why would he leave his house to Victoria instead of his own daughter?*

Josie drained half the cup and then said, "You don't believe in ghosts, do you? I mean when people die they die, right? Of course they do." She waved a hand at me and drained the rest of her cup. "Listen to me sitting here blabbering on." She looked at me and patted my hand. "You're real nice. I need to go but hey, I don't know many people here. Let's do drinks one night, all right?" She threw her oversized leather bag over her shoulder and tugged on her tight skirt.

"Sure, Josie. You know where to find me." I went to unlock the door for her.

"You take good care of Goldie now." She turned back to me. "You don't want Victoria coming back to give you hell." She snorted at her own joke and wiggled her fingers at me before making her way onto the sidewalk with a slight wobble to her walk.

I locked the door behind her and leaned against it, staring at Charlie.

"Just wow," Charlie said, shaking her head.

CHAPTER NINE

Will had a few hours free Saturday afternoon, so he picked me up and we headed to the dog show at Azalea Park. We were following up on my idea that Goldie may have been the real target. Will thought it was a solid idea, and it couldn't hurt to ask some questions. I understood that letting me tag along was a big concession on his part, and I was grateful. Usually he was telling me to mind my own business when it came to sleuthing.

My thumb played with the promise ring he had given me, twirling it around on my finger as I stared out the car window. I glanced over at him. He seemed more preoccupied than normal, biting the inside of his cheek.

"Penny for your thoughts," I said.

He threw me a soft smile and moved his hand from the steering wheel to my thigh. "I'm just a little worried about my dad. He hasn't been feeling good and is going in for some heart tests on Monday."

I placed my hand on top of his and squeezed. "I'm sure everything will be fine. Even if they find a problem, medicine really can work miracles these days." I stayed away from the word "magic".

"Yeah." He flipped his hand over and intertwined our fingers. "I'm sure you're right. Guess I feel guilty, too, because I haven't visited him in awhile."

"Can't you get some time off to go see him this week then?"

He shook his head and then shrugged. "Maybe." Steering the sedan into the park, he glanced in the back seat at Goldie stretched out with Gator between her paws. I glanced at her, too. She seemed to have calmed down from the crazy reaction she had to the magick-infused water, thank heavens. "Let's split up. You walk Goldie around and see if anyone recognizes her and approaches you. That's all you do, understand?" I bit my lip and nodded. "Okay. I'll go ask some official questions."

Will now approved of my snooping? My eyebrows raised but I didn't say anything. I wasn't about to spoil the moment.

He parked, lingered over my mouth a bit longer than a "see you later" kiss warranted and told me he'd find me in a bit.

I grinned, all lit up inside from his touch and then tried to keep my mind on the task at hand. "Okay, focus, Darwin."

I lead Goldie into the park to the open soccer field where the AKC All-Breed dog show was rockin' under large white tents. I supposed the first thing I should do is try to find some other golden retrievers in the show. Their owners would most likely have known Victoria. If dog shows were like any other elite activity, it was a small community with lots of gossip. I just had to find the right person and ask the right questions.

As I approached the crowds, I began to feel a bit underdressed in my white cotton sweatsuit. Most of the women wore black skirts, blazers and sensible shoes with very serious expressions. A nod and a smile only got me a nod back.

After making our way past a few of the tents with no golden retrievers prancing around in the show rings, I led Goldie over to the backside of the tents, where tables had been set up and people in aprons were grooming their dogs.

Scanning the area, I finally spotted a few goldens getting their beauty treatment. I moseyed over to a teenager trimming the whiskers off a stunning golden standing on the table.

"That's a beauty of a dog you got there. How do you get her to stand so calm like that?"

The girl glanced my way and smiled down at Goldie. No recognition. She laughed before resuming her delicate procedure. "She's a diva, used to being fussed over. She loves it."

"What girl wouldn't, right?" I laughed. "So, how long have you been showing her?"

"Not long. I'm actually in the Junior Showmanship classes, so I'm the one getting judged, not Princess here." She pointed her comb over to a golden getting groomed three tables down. "Good thing cause that golden over there is Blackbeard's Bountiful Treasure. Impossible to beat right now."

Guess that would be someone I needed to talk to. "Well, good luck to you and Princess."

"Thanks."

I led Goldie over to the dog she had pointed out. "Beautiful golden," I said, standing to the side. "Is he yours?"

The lady in the apron didn't glance up from the dainty foot she was trimming invisible hairs off of. "Nope, I'm just the handler. Bo belongs to Tara Scarpetta." She lowered the dog's paw and rubbed her hand gently along his leg, finally looking up at me, pride evident in her smile. "He's a champion." Then she glanced down at Goldie, her gaze moving to the shaved area exposing her stitches. Her eyes widened. "Oh my god, is that Goldie?"

Bingo. A hit. "Yes."

She fell down in front of the dog, and took her face in her hands. "Oh, you poor thing." She kissed the space between her eyes. Goldie accepted the attention with grace and a few licks of her own. "Terrible, terrible, losing Victoria like that. I'm sure she's traumatized. Goldens are very sensitive creatures. Form strong bonds with their people." She motioned to the shaved area on her side with the stitches. "Is that from the car hitting them?"

"Yeah, doesn't seem to bother her too much. I was told it might hurt her show career, though."

"Probably would. I mean, even if it's not in the rules, some judges might not be willing to overlook such a big scar."

I nodded in understanding. *So, whoever killed Victoria also probably ended Goldie's show career? That was convenient.*

She sniffed as she gave Goldie one last scratch behind the ears and stood, shaking her head. "Poor thing."

"She seems to be a fighter. Getting better every day." I tried to give her thoughtful sadness the space it deserved, but after a moment of silence, I had to ask the question. "So, you knew Victoria?"

"Well, yeah, everybody on the show circuit did. Victoria and Goldie were a great team, giving Bo here a run for his money."

"I'm kind of new to this whole show world. Can I ask what kind of atmosphere these competitions have? Are they friendly rivalries?"

The woman snorted as she ran a comb through Bo's shiny fur. The dog shifted his curious gaze to me, and I noted the signature sparkle in his eyes.

"You remember high school? All the gossip, rumors, backstabbing?"

Not really. I never went to a public school, but to keep her talking I nodded.

"Well, it's like that but with more money, power, politics and teeth. And I'm not talking about the dog's teeth, either."

I crossed my arms. "That doesn't sound very friendly. So, Victoria and Bo's owner—this Tara Scarpetta—they didn't get along?"

She shook her head. "That's an understatement." She glanced around and lowered her voice. "They were always accusing each other of sabotaging the other's wins."

"How would they do that?"

"Well, you didn't hear this from me and no one could prove it, of course, but Bo got really bad diarrhea before his last show at the Boca Kennel Club and Tara swears Victoria poisoned him."

I stared at her. "That can't be true, can it? I mean, Victoria loved dogs, she wouldn't harm one."

She shrugged. "Victoria loved *her* dog. And winning." Then she sighed. "Tara can be a little dramatic, but I don't think she'd say something like that if she didn't believe it was true."

I glanced down at Goldie. *Just how important was winning to Victoria? Important enough to make an enemy out of someone she didn't realize was dangerous?* "Is Tara here today?"

"Yeah, she's around here somewhere."

I reached out and stroked Bo's soft fur. "Thanks for the help and good luck today."

She nodded and gave Goldie one last scratch before her attention was back on Bo.

I circled around the grounds looking for Will. It would probably be a better idea for him to talk to Tara officially, in case she turned out to be a suspect. I didn't want to mess anything up.

Finally spotting him talking to a couple of serious looking men in suits, I stood off to the side and waved to get his attention.

Ending his conversation with handshakes, he walked over. "What's up?"

"I found Victoria's rival. Probably be a good idea to have a chat with her if you can find her here. Apparently, she believes Victoria poisoned her dog, Bo, at a recent show."

He leaned back on his heels and smiled at me. "Good work. What's her name?"

I felt my cheeks warm at his compliment. "Tara Scarpetta."

Tara wasn't hard to find. Seemed everyone knew her. Will approached her as she was heavy in conversation with another woman, her hands on her slender hips, a scowl barely concealed behind dark glasses.

I stayed back with Goldie and watched the dogs prance around the ring in front of us. A playful collie caught my eye and made me smile. I was still close enough to listen in on Will's conversation, though. I wasn't eavesdropping, really. I was just saving him from having to repeat it over again.

He flashed his badge as he approached the women and asked to speak to Tara privately. The woman she was talking to skedaddled, seemingly relieved.

"Will you remove your glasses, please?"

I smiled to myself. Will believed people's eyes were windows to their souls. He said he liked to stare into mine because he could see right into my beautiful soul. I sighed and glanced over at them. Victoria had removed her glasses and now stood glaring at him with her arms crossed over her black blazer.

"What's this about, Detective?" Her voice held more than a hint of irritation.

It didn't seem to faze him. "I'm sure you've heard about Victoria Desoto-Roth's death?"

"Yes, of course."

"What was your relationship with her?"

Her snort of laughter was filled with spite. "We had no relationship, Detective."

"Just a rivalry?"

"We were both competing in the same shows, so yes, a rivalry."

"A friendly one?"

I cut my eyes back their way and saw her move her hands to her hips.

"No. Not a particularly friendly one. What is this about?"

"What kind of car do you drive?"

She took a moment to answer. "A Mercedes."

"Color?"

More hesitation. "Black."

"Where were you last Saturday evening, around six o'clock?"

I watched as she stared into the show ring, her mouth set in a hard line. She turned back to Will. "This is starting to sound like you are accusing me of having something to do with Victoria's death. Are you?"

"Do you have something you'd like to tell me?"

She smiled then, but it wasn't a friendly smile. "If you have any more questions for me, Detective, I'd like my attorney present."

I glanced at Will. He nodded and pulled out a card from his pocket. "Call me to set up an interview this week with your attorney present then, Miss Scarpetta." He didn't say "or else" but his tone implied it nicely. "Have a good day."

He walked over to me. "I think we're done here."

I nodded and began to follow him back to the car. One last glance behind me sent a chill up my spine. Tara still stood in the spot Will left her, her arms crossed and her glare focused on Goldie.

I turned to Will. With the way Tara reacted, it couldn't hurt to ask. "You didn't happen to notice if Tara was wearing perfume, did you? Something that smelled like lilacs?"

He shook his head. "Didn't notice, sorry."

I glanced back one more time. She had her cell phone out, but was still staring at us.

CHAPTER TEN

Just before closing time on Friday, Frankie came in with a box of something trailing a lemon scent. "TGIF, gals!"

"You said it, Frankie." I collapsed in the chair and peeked in the box. Lemon tarts. *Yum.*

"Anything interesting today?" I asked, taking a sip of tea and smiling at Charlie as she patiently waited on a customer who was explaining he wasn't really yelling, his hearing aids were just on the fritz.

"Naw, same old... oh, wait." Frankie chuckled. "Here's something good in the *Gossip Around Town* section. The St. Pete Paranormal Society says they were conducting an investigation this past week of the 1,000-year-old American Indian burial and temple Mound at Pinellas Point last weekend and caught some light anomalies on film. The next day, neighbors of the Mound reported it had been vandalized, part of it dug up."

"Oh yeah, I met some ladies who live across the street from there and they mentioned that. They also said one of their husbands was conked on the head with a shovel while patrolling the area, trying to stop the vandalism." I thought about Willow and how this story was right up her alley. I still remember the home schooling reports she did on the American Indians, one of her favorite subjects to this day.

"Probably some kids looking for Indian trinkets." Frankie sighed. "No respect now days."

That would make sense, except for the fact it wasn't a kid but an adult that conked the guy on the head with a shovel. Maybe even a woman. *That's it.* I needed to visit this Mound. It was turning into a hub of activity. Activity that may be connected to Victoria's death.

Frankie snapped her fingers, her eyes lighting up as she fished her cell phone out of her bag. "Hey, I just remembered my masseuse, Veronica, telling me she's a member of this ghost hunting team. I'll call her and get the scoop."

I took the opportunity to finish up some closing-time chores as Frankie chatted. When I returned to the tea table, she was grinning at me mischievously.

"Guess what?"

I was afraid to ask but I knew she'd tell me anyway. "What?"

"Turns out the St. Pete Paranormal Society is investigating there again tonight to try and capture more evidence on video."

"And?" I asked, even though I knew what was coming.

"And she invited me along. What do you say? Want to go see about some ghosts?"

I grabbed another tart and licked lemon filling off my fingers. Her eyes were sparkling. How could I say no? She's never said no to me on any of the crazy adventures I dragged her along on. Besides, I did just decide I needed to go there. "All right. I'm game. I don't want to leave Goldie alone, though. You think it's all right if she tags along?"

Frankie shrugged. "I don't see why not. I don't think I've heard a peep out of her since you've had her. Don't think she'll bother anybody."

I nodded. She had seemed sad again this morning. Guess she'll have her ups and downs like any of us. "Yeah, I'd actually love to see her get excited and bark at something."

We headed down 1-275 in Frankie's little red sports car with Goldie crammed in the back. I secretly wished it wasn't too chilly to have the top down. There was something freeing about riding in a car with the top down. Plus, it was the only saving grace from feeling like a sardine in this car.

I watched a truck speed by us. Everyone's always in a hurry. "What's the story with this Indian Mound anyway?"

"Well, it's the surviving burial Mound from a Tocobaga Indian Village that was there like a thousand years ago. It was occupied for about six hundred years until the Spanish explorers came. Some folks believe it was this very site that inspired the story of Pocahontas. The real story is about a Spanish sailor, Juan Ortiz, being saved from certain death by the Chief's daughter."

"That's kind of romantic. Were they in love?"

"Naw. I think he became her servant. How's that for a twist? Disney won't be making that version of the story any time soon." Frankie chuckled as she steered her car smoothly off the Pinellas Point Drive exit.

"I can't even imagine what life was like around here back then."

"In a wild, untamed Florida? Me neither." Frankie adjusted the air vent. "I'm happy living in my air conditioning with scheduled pest control."

I laughed. "Well, I'm sure you appreciate it more than most."

We drove down the residential streets to find quite a few cars parked along the street that bordered the Mound.

"No parking area?" I asked, surprised.

"Nope. But, I'm sure the folks who live here are used to visitors parking in their street." Frankie pulled two flashlights out of the glove box and handed me one with a grin as I helped Goldie leap out of the back seat. "Let's go hunt us some ghosts."

I scanned the large green metal sign with the rules as we entered. Nothing said 'no dogs allowed'. That was good. We picked our way deeper into the Mound, following the narrow beam of our flashlights. Crushed shells, pine needles and leaves crunched under our feet. I was surprised at how peaceful it was, considering we were there to capture evidence of a ghost.

We spotted a faint light at the top of the hill.

"Up there." Frankie motioned with her flash light. "Let's just head up this path instead of going around to the back steps."

Goldie and I climbed the gently sloping earth behind her. At the top, it flattened out a bit. Small palm trees and other vegetation had grown in the soil. Spanish moss hung from a large oak tree, its thick branches reaching out over the area like guardians. The scent of wet leaves, moist earth and burning sage greeted us.

A few bodies were huddled under a stretched out oak branch, a small lantern glowing between them.

A woman waved at us. "Over here."

We made our way over to the group and Frankie introduced me to Veronica, her masseuse. Veronica introduced us to the other team members.

"Nice to meet y'all." I took a seat on the chilly earth. Goldie sniffed the ground, turned a circle and lay down against my leg with a sigh.

Off to our left, I spotted yellow tape roping off an area in a small square. Veronica noticed my attention on it.

"That's where someone dug up the ground," she offered. "It was a pretty deep hole from what I heard. The neighbors filled it in best they could. Not sure why they left the tape up? Though, I know the Spirit Tribe is coming to do some kind of ceremony, to restore peace to their ancestors who might have been disturbed. Maybe they left it up so the Spirit Tribe would know where the Mound was disturbed."

I nodded. *That was thoughtful of them.* "Who are the Spirit Tribe?"

"They're an intertribal group of folks trying to keep their ancestors' memories and way of life from dying." She ran a hand through her short cropped hair. "I think they'll be here tonight, so you'll be able to meet them if you stay."

If I stay? Was she expecting me to run off if the ghost showed up? I smiled. "I wish my sister, Willow, was here. She'd be in heaven if she could meet them. So, Veronica, do you think someone could be digging up the Mound searching for artifacts to sell?"

"I guess it's possible. I'm sure there are people around who don't respect what this Mound stands for, what it is. Artifacts are a big business and people are greedy."

Just then I noticed one of the guys, introduced as Bob, was holding a piece of equipment with a tiny green flashing light.

"What's that for?" I asked.

"Looks like a TV remote," Frankie snorted.

"This is an EMF detector," he explained. "If there are any fluctuations in the EMF field, I'll start recording. Maybe we'll get lucky tonight and catch us a voice."

I listened to the breeze and a shiver went through me. It seemed to carry a low growl our way. Probably just my imagination.

"There you go, a spike," Veronica whispered, nodding at the EMF meter as a whole row of green and red lights lit up.

Bob quickly pulled a video camera out of a silver case and flicked it on. "Is someone here with us?" We all listened intently. "Are you the spirit who showed yourself to us the other night?"

Veronica chimed in with her own question. "Can you manifest yourself again or talk to us?"

He stood and panned the camera around the area. "Are you here to guard this Mound? Are you angry someone desecrated this sacred space?"

There was a rustling behind us, and we all turned and peered into the darkness. It didn't go unnoticed by me that Goldie didn't move. Probably a squirrel.

Another member, introduced to us as Cassidy, had stood and began walking around taking flash pictures of the area. I stroked Goldie's fur absentmindedly as I watched her. Then I leaned over to Veronica, "Aren't y'all worried the spirits, or whatever they are, aren't going to be friendly?"

She shrugged. "We're protected."

Just then, the recorder playing the Indian chants in the background quit. Goldie raised her head. We both looked down at her. Her ears were pushed high on her head in an alert position, and she was staring intently at the guy taking the pictures. A low growl began in her throat.

"Dogs can be very sensitive to spirit energy," Veronica whispered, excitement crackling in her voice.

"Whoa!" Bob turned back to us. "Heavy EMF spike."

"Why'd the recorder stop? Think it's the ghost?" Frankie tried to whisper, but she wasn't very good at it. Her voice still cut through the air.

The guy taking pictures froze as a hot breeze swept over the area.

Whatever insects and frogs had been chirping went still. The silence was deafening. The air grew thick. Everyone's breathing sounded loud. Goldie whimpered and looked up at me. I wrapped my arms around her body and held her close.

"Oh my god!" Bob yelped, whipping around and stumbling down the slope.

A few heartbeats later, the air seemed to cool and return to normal. Goldie rested her head on my lap.

"It's gone." Bob rushed back up to us and went to the recorder. "Batteries are drained."

Veronica stood and dusted off her jeans. "Dang, those were brand new."

"Well, that was odd. Spirit energy is usually cold." Cassidy approached the team.

"Did you see anything?" Frankie asked.

"Yes." Bob cast his glance about the Mound nervously. "You guys are going to think I'm nuts, but I think it was a dog. We'll have to see if we caught anything on video."

"A dog?" Cassidy asked. "What kind of dog?"

"A big one. But it was more like I was seeing a dog's shadow except..." He put his hands on his hips. "Except I swear I caught a glimpse of red eyes."

They all looked at each other. I glanced around to make sure some red-eyed shadow dog wasn't about to pounce on us.

"Wow." Veronica squeezed his arm. "Well, like you said, we'll have to check the video. Maybe we caught something."

CHAPTER ELEVEN

We all turned as we heard soft footfalls coming toward us. Three figures climbed the hill and emerged from the shadows. They weren't carrying any flashlights or lanterns but Bob swung a lantern toward them. Two women and a man approached.

"Evening," the shorter woman said, raising a hand in greeting. A cloth bag hung off one shoulder and her long, inky hair was pulled back into a low ponytail. The man with her was much older with gray hair and a quiet demeanor.

"Hey." Veronica moved forward and held out her hand. "You must be the Spirit Tribe folks."

"Yes. Jade Harjo." She shook her hand. "This is my daughter, Kimi." She motioned to the woman standing behind her with her arms crossed. She was taller and thinner but had the same inky dark hair pulled away from her face.

"Oh." I sat up straighter. "Jade Harjo?"

She turned to me and peered through the darkness. "Yes?" Coming closer, she made a little gasp of surprise. "Is that Goldie?"

Goldie's tail thumped twice in response, and she lifted her head off my lap as the woman bent down to stroke her ears.

"Yes it is. I'm adopting her. I'm Darwin." I shook her hand. "You were Victoria's friend, weren't you? I'm so sorry for your loss."

She looked up into my face, her dark eyes shining above a sad smile. "Thank you. You knew Victoria?"

"No, not really. My boyfriend, Detective Blake, is the one who pulled Goldie out of the Bay the night Victoria was killed. He got the call about the accident. He's a homicide detective." I could feel everyone's attention on me and knew I should stop talking, but the story kept pouring out. "The clinic called me the next morning and said Victoria's husband didn't want to take Goldie back and would I be willing to adopt her."

"Eugene didn't want her?" Her voice was heavy with sadness. She whispered something to Goldie in a language I didn't know. "But why?"

"Apparently he's too traumatized. Can't even barely take care of himself. In his defense, he does look awful."

"Selfish," she said softly. "Always has been. Victoria couldn't have children. This soul was her child. To just turn her away, deny her the comfort of her home..." she choked on the words.

"I know, but I can't say I'm not happy to have her with me. You were meeting Victoria that night, weren't you? That must have been such a shock."

"Yes. It's still hard to believe she's gone."

"Were you good friends?"

"I am... was a long time friend of Renny Desoto, Victoria's uncle who recently passed. Victoria was like a second daughter to me."

Her daughter, Kimi, said something in a harsh tone I didn't understand.

Jade threw her a quick look and then continued. "In fact, that's why we were meeting. She wanted to give me an artifact she found while cleaning out Renny's attic after he passed. Something she was very excited about over the phone, but she wouldn't tell me what it was. She wanted it to be a surprise. Renny collected all kinds of Native American treasures, and I guess she wanted to make sure this particular one came back to us instead of being sold by Eugene's friend, Big Barnie, at his artifact shop."

Barnie? That was the second time someone had mentioned his name to me. And he knew Victoria? I was getting the feeling he was involved somehow.

"Renny and Eugene had more than a few arguments over giving the artifacts to Big Barnie to make a profit. Renny understood how much these things mean to my people." She paused. "Funny thing is, your Detective Blake showed me the artifact, and I was a bit confused. It was a fairly nice beveled arrowhead but not something to get so excited about."

I knew nothing about artifacts or Victoria, so I didn't know what to think. I did know one person in their family, though. "I met Renny's daughter, Josie. She came to my pet boutique Wednesday night to see Goldie."

Kimi scoffed and walked away.

Jade watched her daughter leave and shook her head. "Trouble, that one. Renny named her after Jose Gaspar, the pirate. He wanted a boy." She smiled almost sadly. "Renny's great-great-grandfather supposedly pirated with Gaspar back in the 1900's. I told him not to name a child after a pirate. It was just asking for trouble."

I watched the investigators pack up their gear. "Well, she seemed real... nice."

"Mmm. Maybe just lost." She leaned over and planted a kiss on Goldie's nose. "Thank you for taking her in, Darwin. Looks like she's already attached to you. Victoria would be happy to know she's in a loving home."

As she stood, I heard Bob talking to the man with the thin, gray braid down his back. The man was explaining how this was their ancestors' sacred resting place and that's why they would try to restore peace to the disturbed ground.

I stood, too, catching Bob's question to the man. "So, you believe a ghost dog could be the Mound's guardian spirit?"

He nodded and patted Bob's arm. "We believe everyone has a guardian spirit. But, Westerners ignore nature and her power so what can the spirits do?"

I smiled at Jade. "Well, we should let you get started. It was real nice meeting you. Feel free to come by Darwin's Pet Boutique any time and visit Goldie. I'm sure any friends from her old life can only help her heal."

We all said our goodbyes and then followed the investigators off of the Mound.

CHAPTER TWELVE

Frankie pulled her leopard print wrap tighter around her shoulders and shoved her fingers into her spiky red hair to fluff it. "So fill me in why you arranged this dinner again."

"Because of Victoria. Josie is her cousin and she might hold some clue as to who killed her, whether she knows it or not. Thanks for coming with me, by the way. Are you cold?" I pulled my own sweater in around my neck. "I can run Goldie upstairs, and we can eat inside if you want."

"No, no." She lifted her glass of merlot. "I'll have one more of these and be toasty warm." She smiled down at Goldie, lying between our chairs with her snout on her paws. Her own dogs were warm and cozy in the buggy next to her. "Besides, she needs to know you're not going to abandon her. Goldens are people dogs. They don't like to be alone."

I thought about the mess in my bedroom. "I've noticed." I lifted my own glass of merlot. "Cheers to that and staying warm." We clinked glasses with a shared smile. I took a sip and then said, "So apparently, Victoria's Uncle Renny died and Josie—Renny's daughter—came here for the funeral. She lives in Vegas and I hate to judge her, but I'm pretty sure she's an alcoholic."

Just then, Goldie lifted her head. We followed her stare to see Josie climbing out of a cab, none too elegantly. She glanced around, spotted us and weaved her way through the crowd.

"Hey, Darwin." She greeted me with a large smile, then leaned down and scratched Goldie's head. "How's our girl doing?"

"She's doing all right," I said absentmindedly, because as Josie had bent down, the scent of lilacs wafted toward me. *What did that mean? Should I consider the lilac scent a clue once again?* I forced a smile. "Josie, this is my friend, Frankie."

Josie straightened up, wobbling a bit on her pink heels and shook Frankie's hand. "Nice to meet you, Frankie." Her gaze moved to the five carat diamond on the hand she was holding. "Holy crap, is that real?"

Frankie shot her an amused look. "That it is, darling. Why don't you have a seat?" I caught her mumbling, "Before you fall down."

Josie plopped into a chair, flipping her long hair over one shoulder. "Thanks for hanging with me tonight, girls. Victoria used to hang out with me when I visited. Damn, I sure miss her."

"I'm sorry for your loss, Josie," Frankie offered. "Darwin was telling me you also lost your father recently?"

"Yeah. I mean, that wasn't such a shock, you know, he was old. But, Victoria—" She shook her head. "She was in the prime of her life, just starting to cut loose and enjoy herself."

"What do you mean?" I shifted uncomfortably. It felt wrong gossiping about someone who'd passed, but if her death was foul play, she deserved to have the person caught. Any information that could lead to that wasn't really gossip in my book. Besides, this is what I wanted from Josie... the inside scoop.

Our waiter came by and Josie ordered a Coke. Then she scanned the tables around us, leaned her elbows on the table and motioned for us to move in closer. "She wasn't happy with Eugene. I mean, who could be happy with a guy named Eugene, right?" she scoffed. Then she waved that thought off. "She was in love with Eugene's best friend and they finally started... you know... hooking up." Her penciled eyebrows rose high over glassy brown eyes.

Frankie and I shared a confused look as we all leaned back in our chairs.

"Josie, are you talking about Big Barnie?" I asked.

"Yeah." She frowned. "You know him?"

"No." I shook my head. *But, it's about time I did.* "I met a good friend of your father's though, Jade Harjo. She mentioned something about your dad and Eugene disagreeing on giving your father's Indian artifacts to Big Barnie to sell in his shop. That Victoria also wanted them to go to Jade."

Josie's eyes narrowed. "Huh. I have a hard time imagining that. Victoria would have done anything for Barnie." A look crossed her face I couldn't decipher. "Eugene and Barnie are having some big fight. I think it's because Eugene found out about them. I can't imagine anything else coming between them. They've been best friends since they were kids."

The waiter brought Josie's Coke and we ordered. After he left, she dug through her bag and pulled out a flask.

"Didn't realize this was bring your own booze night," Frankie teased.

"A gal's gotta save money where she can." Josie shrugged, pouring a generous dollop from the flask into her Coke, eyeing Frankie sideways. "I don't suppose you need to worry about that though."

I saw Frankie's face color and she raised an eyebrow at me. "Guess I asked for that one."

Frankie had lived in Pirate City for a long time before she won the lottery. The place was dangerous and not for the faint of heart. Snide remarks about her not knowing what it was to be poor were never well received by her. I rested my hand on Frankie's arm, hoping to bring her down to a simmer. She took a breath and a swallow of merlot, then gave me a nod. She was okay.

"So, Josie." I changed the subject. "Your father, did he have a lot of Indian artifacts?"

"I guess." She shrugged. "His attic was full of junk. He was into all that Indian and pirate stuff. Supposedly my great-great," she paused, staring at her hand, then lifted another finger slowly, "great-granddaddy pirated with Gasparilla. That's how come there's a pirate skull on the tattoo I got in his memory." She lifted the sleeve of her sweater and showed Frankie. Then she drained half her glass, sending the ice clinking against her teeth. "I'm just grateful Victoria cleared it all out after he died. One less thing for me to do, whether I sell the house or live in it."

"Wow, that's some family history. Is that why he named you after a pirate?" I asked.

She shook her head in disgust. "Yeah, Jose Gasper... aka Gasparilla, in fact. He really wanted a boy."

"Gasparilla's just a legend, isn't it?" Frankie leaned back as the waiter came with our meals. After he served us, he placed a bowl of boiled chicken and cooked carrots on the ground for Goldie. She pushed herself up off the ground and dug in enthusiastically.

I smiled at the waiter. "Thanks, Rocco."

Josie shrugged. "My dad didn't think so. Told folks he had proof Gasparilla was real but when anyone would ask him to put his money where his mouth was, he'd just grin and wink at 'em." She frowned and looked at us sideways. "Anyways, he was just a crazy old man. Victoria was a real sweetheart, though. She didn't think it was right daddy didn't leave me the house. She told me she'd changed her will immediately so I'd have it. Just didn't think I'd be getting it so soon."

I shared a frown with Frankie.

"Your dad sounds like he was an interesting character." Frankie took a bite of steak and chewed thoughtfully. "So, what do you do out there in Vegas?"

"I work a roulette table at the Luxor. Tips are good." She pushed her salad around with her fork and stared at the night traffic, sighing. "Just not good enough."

"Is it expensive to live there?" I asked.

She nodded. "In more ways than one. But then, it's expensive to live here, too. You know Victoria left most of her family money, and believe me she had plenty of it, to the Golden Retriever Rescue. I'm sure Eugene the Bean is pretty sore about that."

"Yeah, I imagine he would be." *Time to bring up the lilac perfume.* "Mm, you know, Josie, I can't help but ask you about that lovely perfume you're wearing."

She sniffed her wrist. "Oh, this old stuff? Victoria gave me a bottle last time I visited. Said Eugene bought her a few bottles for her birthday cause he loved the smell." She shrugged. "I get compliments on it, and it was free. Can't beat that." Then she drained her glass and changed the subject, a dark look passing over her face. "So, Darwin, tell me about the night you rescued Goldie."

CHAPTER THIRTEEN

Usually Sylvia unlocks the front door and strolls through with a bright smile, a "*Bom dia*!" and a box full of sweet, sticky treats. Not today. Nope, today she busted through the door, squealing and closing the distance between us surprisingly quickly in her two inch heels before she attacked me, grabbing me and jumping up and down, spinning me in circles. I found myself screaming, then laughing at her huge grin and tear-filled brown eyes. Goldie actually pushed herself up and sat there staring at us with her tongue hanging out. I think she was laughing, too.

"Sylvia!" I tried to catch my breath. "What in heaven's name has happened?"

She just squealed and thrust her left hand in front of my face. A huge, square diamond almost poked me in the eye.

"Holy heaven on a stick!" I grabbed her hand, moving it away from my eye so I could actually focus on it. "That is gorgeous! Is that... does this mean... are you and Landon engaged?"

She nodded, breathless, throwing her hand to her heart over her red silk blouse. "Oh, it was so *romântico*! He made me come up to the stage at his show last night. Then there was all this smoke, it cleared and Mage was sitting in front of me with a rose in his mouth. The ring, it was on the rose. Landon dropped to one knee in front of the whole crowd."

Mage was Landon's black German shepherd. I've seen him use Mage in his magic acts before, but I was sorry I missed this one. "Oh, that is romantic! What did he say?"

"Honestly, I was in such shock, I don't remember the words. Just his eyes, so full of emotion and his hand was shaking as he took mine. I remember, 'Will you be my wife?' and I cry as I say, 'Of course'. He puts the ring on my finger. We kiss and the crowd stands with shouts, whistles, clapping. Mage is barking. It was like a fairytale."

"Oh, Sylvia." I hugged her tight, wiping at my own eyes. "I'm so happy for you. You guys make the best couple. Congratulations."

The squealing and congratulations commenced once again as two of our regular customers came through the door and joined in the celebration.

The morning flew by amidst all the excitement. I waited until Charlie came to work and asked her to keep an eye on Goldie while I ran an errand. It was time I met this Big Barnie character.

His shop, Treasure Coast Artifacts, wasn't hard to find online. Neither was information on him such as his real name, Barnabus Imbach, his trespassing arrest a few years back, an article on him the *Tribune* did last year and the fact he was fifty years old and never been married. *Is that because he was secretly in love with his best friend's wife?*

The cab dropped me off in front of the shop. I had no idea what I would say to him. It wasn't like I could come right out and say, "So, you and Victoria were having a fling, huh?" Or, "Do you deal in illegally acquired artifacts?" Maybe just seeing what kind of person he was would give me a clue.

The inside of the shop was warm and dry and smelled like dust. I shrugged off my sweater and draped it over my straw bag as I took in the place. It was packed full of glass cases, baskets, bins, shelves and tables that held unearthed treasures of every kind. Foreign music played over the speakers. I moved deeper into the shop, spotting Big Barnie standing in front of the counter chatting with another guy. He looked like the photo that had accompanied the article in the newspaper, though his curly dark hair was a bit grown out. He was a big guy, broad shouldered and had an air of confidence about him. King of his castle. A half dozen other people meandered through the shop.

My eyes roamed over a table of animal skulls and bones. Each had a price tag. One giant bone sat at the back of the table and claimed to be from a mammoth. There were baskets of sharks' teeth and small arrowheads. I moved along the wall, studying the hanging framed glass cases with displays of larger arrowheads and spears. As I moved closer to Barnie, I stopped at a wide glass case and peered in at the fossils inside. A pair of large, blue-white rocks caught my eye because of the $950 price tag. Mammoth molars? Now that was cool. Up in the same price range were a couple of six inch Megladon sharks' teeth. I hadn't realized fossils and artifacts could fetch such a steep price. Interesting.

I heard Big Barnie end his conversation with the guy he had been chatting with, and then he was by my side. His presence felt like a wall. He sure was a big guy. Guess that explained the nickname.

"Anything I can help you with?"

I looked up into cool gray eyes and returned his smile. "My sister lives in Georgia and just loves all things Native American. I was told you could help me out with something to send her for her birthday." Wasn't exactly a lie. I could send Willow an early birthday present.

"You came to the right place, little lady. What price range were you thinking?"

I glanced at the high-priced fossils. "You have anything under fifty dollars?"

He rubbed his meaty hands together and chuckled. "Yes ma'am. Follow me." I followed him over to the counter where he pointed to some jewelry. "I'm assuming you don't want to give her sharks' teeth or arrowheads. This jewelry is crafted by local Native Americans." He unlocked the case and pulled out a few items. "We have spiny oyster shell earrings, beaded necklaces, turquoise bracelets—"

"Oh, she would love that." I pointed to an earthy orange bracelet. "It's her favorite color."

"Ah, good choice." He pulled it from the display case. "Hand painted clay beads." He placed it in my hand.

"It's beautiful. I'll take it, thanks." I handed it back, studying him as he rang up the bracelet. *How to bring up Victoria?* I drummed my fingers on the glass counter and cleared my throat. "I'm so glad Josie recommended your shop to me. I'll have to thank her."

A bushy brow rose as he glanced over at me. "Josie Desoto?"

Was it Desoto? Yes, it must be because that was Victoria's last name. "Yes, you know her?"

"Yeah," he grunted before wrapping the bracelet in tissue paper. Eyeing me with new interest he said, "Real piece of work, that one. How do you know her?"

"Well, kind of a sad story. She came into my boutique. I'm co-owner of Darwin's Pet Boutique on Beach Drive. Anyway, she came in to visit the golden retriever I'm adopting. Her name's Goldie. She belonged to Josie's cousin..." I looked pointedly into his eyes as I said, "Victoria." I wasn't disappointed. His eyes widened and his mood changed instantly. Gone was the laid back shop owner. Something dark and dangerous moved into his gaze.

"Victoria." He repeated, letting his gaze fall. Whether to hide the emotion or just to get it under control, it was too late. I saw it. He definitely had very strong feelings for her. I felt them wash over me in hot waves.

Taking a deep breath, I pushed through his emotions, staying aware they weren't mine and letting them pass. "Such a tragedy, what happened. So, you knew her. Victoria?"

"Yeah." He bagged up the bracelet, no longer meeting my eye. "Eugene, her husband and I have been good friends since high school. Grew up together. She... she was a great gal. How is Goldie doing? Victoria sure loved that dog."

"She seems a little less sad every day." He nodded. I handed him my debit card. "Such a small world. I'm glad Eugene has a friend. Seems like he needs one right now. He doesn't seem to be handling his wife's passing too well."

"No," he frowned and shook his head, "he doesn't." He handed me back my card, the package and a receipt and forced a smile. "Have yourself a nice day, Miss Winters."

CHAPTER FOURTEEN

Frankie insisted on having an engagement party for Sylvia and Landon and after the busy week we had, I knew Sylvia was ready to let her hair down and have some fun. I talked Frankie into inviting Josie so I could find out more about her relationship with Victoria. I had come to the conclusion that if there was somebody capable of driving drunk and hitting a person, she was a good candidate. I hated to think ill of her, but I couldn't ignore the facts either. Plus she had motive. She inherited her dad's house after Victoria died. And I couldn't ignore the lilac perfume. I owed Frankie a favor now, seeing as how she wasn't too fond of Josie, but she finally agreed.

The elevator doors opened up into Frankie's five-thousand-square-foot penthouse that took up the entire top floor of the Vinoy Towers. "Wow!" I whispered. On a normal day the place was impressive with its expanse of cherry wood floors, marble fireplace, crystal chandeliers and leather furnishing. Not to mention the fact the entire front wall was glass with a view of water and sky. But tonight, she had outdone herself.

A champagne fountain sat in front of the windows. The furniture had been rearranged to allow for a lighted dance floor with a live D.J. off in the corner. Dozens of enormous white rose bouquets made the place smell like heaven. Black and white paper lanterns hung from the ceiling, providing soft, romantic lighting. It was breathtaking.

"Darwin!" Frankie waved me over from across the room. Her "small" party looked like it already held over fifty people and the guests of honor hadn't even arrived yet. I made my way over to her, smiling and stopping to say howdy to some of the ladies who were regular customers of the pet boutique.

"There you are, sugar." Frankie hugged me, being careful not to disturb her red sequined and feather hat which matched her red sequined and feathered dress. The look would have been tacky on anyone else, but it was classic Frankie and worked for her. "Where's Will?"

"He'll be here later. He's got some things to wrap up before he can come out and play."

"That man works too hard," she said. Then turning to Veronica, she added, teasing me. "Darwin's caught herself a hunky homicide detective."

"That's right. I remember you saying that at the Mound. Detective Blake, right? Not a single gal in St. Pete who doesn't know who he is. You guys found that poor woman's dog after she got killed? I heard it was a possible drunk driver."

I grabbed a glass of champagne off one of the waiters' trays. "Yeah, that's the most popular theory right now. A drunk driver." I didn't mention

Tara Scarpetta being the number one suspect. I had no idea who her friends were and didn't want her tipped off.

"Speaking of Goldie, you didn't bring her tonight?" Frankie asked.

I swallowed a sip of the bubbly and pointed down at my black cocktail dress. "I didn't think fur would compliment my outfit."

"Good point." Frankie grinned and then turned to Veronica. "Oh, hey, tell Darwin what you were saying about what happened at the Indian Mound again."

She pulled on the hem of her short skirt and shook her head. "More vandalism."

"Guess the ghost dog's not really doing his job guarding the place," Frankie chuckled.

I grinned at Frankie and then thought about all the artifacts at Big Barnie's shop. "I still think it could be someone looking for arrowheads or other things to sell."

Veronica shook her head. "I just don't know. Archeologists have been over the Mound already. It was a temple or burial site. I don't think there's anything of value there. Mostly shell tools were found."

I took a sip of bubbly and thought about that. *But, did they dig deep enough?*

Frankie adjusted her diamond bracelets. "Oh, hey, did you get anything on the video from the night we were all there?"

"Nope." She pressed her lips together. "A few strange noises at the time that hot breeze came through, but nothing definitive."

"Must be hard to get real evidence," I said. "Too bad we don't know who the vandals are. If there is a ghost dog guarding the Mound, he'd for sure show himself to them."

Our conversation was interrupted by applause as Sylvia and Landon stepped out of the elevator. Brandon kissed Sylvia's cheek as she laughed and they both gave a playful bow. They looked stunning, their dark features standing out against coordinated outfits.

"She's going to be a beautiful bride," Frankie said.

A waiter brought them champagne and then they made their way through the crowd, shaking hands and getting hugs and congratulations.

"Oh, wait until you get a load of the cake I got." Frankie grinned. "Chocolate mint with Crème de menthe chocolate mousse and dark chocolate ganache."

I groaned. "You're going to put us all in a sugar coma, Frankie." If I didn't have such a fast metabolism I would have gained fifty pounds between Frankie and Sylvia's love of sweets.

"Death by chocolate and champagne." Veronica giggled. "Now there's a way to go."

The happy couple finally made their way over to us. Sylvia's eyes sparkled through some silky strands all the hugging had knocked loose from her up-do. Landon looked handsome as ever in black slacks and a maroon silk shirt that matched the flowers on Sylvia's black satin dress.

"Congratulations, Landon." I gave him a hug. "You're a lucky guy."

"I know." He grinned. "I still can't believe she said yes."

Sylvia smacked his arm playfully. "Of course I say yes. And Frankie, thank you so much for this party. You've really outdone yourself. It is *estupendo*," she breathed, giving Frankie a tight hug.

Frankie beamed. "You two deserve it. Now go get yourselves some food and dance your feet off!"

It was almost ten o'clock when Will finally showed up. He looked exhausted. I frowned and immediately led him out on the balcony, away from the raucous of the party.

He slipped his arms around me, and I felt cocooned in warmth that seeped right into my heart.

Pressing his lips into my hair I heard him take a deep breath. "I missed you."

I tilted my chin up and looked into his eyes. "What's wrong?"

"Just been a long day." He laid his palm against my cheek and planted a light kiss on my lips. "The moonlight suits you."

"Don't change the subject," I whispered.

He pressed his forehead against mine, and I could feel his weariness. "Sit down. Let me go get you a plate and a drink." I led him to a chair. "Be right back."

I slipped back into the party and fixed Will a plate piled with things I couldn't even pronounce and grabbed him a cold Corona. When I came back out, he had his head leaned back against the chair and his eyes closed.

"Can't really enjoy the view with your eyes shut," I teased him.

He smiled, then accepted the beer while I set the plate on the table beside him.

"So, is it the Victoria Desoto case that's got you so exhausted?"

He swallowed a swig of beer and nodded. "Tara Scarpetta came in for the interview tonight. Doesn't have an alibi for the evening. Says she was home alone. We've got experts going over her car to see if there's any evidence of recent impact."

"She could have already had it repaired, right?"

"Yeah. We've also got someone working on calling all the repair shops in the area to see if anyone has recently brought in a black car with front end damage."

We sat in silence for a moment, then I said, "Victoria's cousin, Josie Desoto is here. She's a real trip. You might want to have a chat with her. She drinks like a fish and apparently she only inherited her father's house after Victoria died. So, there's motive." I didn't mention the lilac perfume. Will wouldn't consider that evidence.

Will glanced at me and then stared out at the dark water. The sky was full of clouds so only a few stars peeked through. "Yeah. We checked into the victim's will. Seems she left most of her money— apparently old money which she had a lot of—to the Golden Retriever Rescue. Left just enough to her husband for him to survive. Also, just days before her death she changed it to leave Josie Desoto the house her uncle had left her. So I had Miss Josie on the interview list." He was lost in thought for a moment and then took a deep breath, blowing it out. "You say she's here?"

I almost wished she wasn't now. Will didn't seem up to talking to her. "Yeah."

He sighed. "Guess I could do an informal interview."

I nodded, handing him the plate. "You put something in your stomach. I'll go get her."

I found Josie on the dance floor teaching a few of our customers some dance moves. She was barefoot and her hair had fallen from its clip.

"Hey, Josie."

She smiled and gave me a sweaty hug. "There you are. Come dance with us!"

I pulled away and grabbed her hand. "No, no. Come take a breather outside. I want you to meet my boyfriend, Will."

"Oh, okay." Her smile grew and she nodded. "I could use a break." She turned to the women. "Carry on, ladies. Shake those moneymakers."

She grabbed a glass of champagne on the way out to the balcony. "Oh, this breeze is just heavenly."

I was suddenly glad she was barefoot as she stumbled over to the curved glass barrier that stopped her from tumbling down into the bay. My heart jumped. I glanced at Will. He raised an eyebrow at me and wiped his fingers off on a napkin.

Moving her away from the balcony to a chair, I said, "Josie, this is Will. Will this is Victoria's cousin, Josie."

"Nice to meet you." She plopped down in the chair, spilling some of the champagne on her dress and shook Will's outstretched hand. "Did you know Victoria?"

I wondered how Will was going to play this. I wasn't sure if she was going to remember that Will was a homicide detective.

He didn't reveal much in his answer. "I've met her husband, Eugene. I'm sorry for your family's loss."

She snorted and gulped her drink. "Thanks."

I tried to move the conversation along for both their sakes. "Josie lost her father, Renny, recently, too. She came here from Las Vegas for his funeral."

Will was staring at her intently. I don't think she noticed though, her eyes were unfocused and pointed toward the dark waters.

"How long after your father's funeral did you lose Victoria?"

"Four days." Ice clinked against Josie's teeth as she drained her glass. "Four, three, two, one... boom." She barked out laughter suddenly.

Will and I shared a concerned look and then he asked, "Where were you the night she got killed, Josie?"

"Where? Where was I?" She rolled her head toward us and her eyes narrowed. "You sound like a cop." Then she smiled, but it wasn't friendly. "Oh yeah, I remember, you are a cop." She shrugged. "I was out. At a club. I suppose you want an alibi? Sorry, I don't remember his name. Cheap bastard. Only bought the cheap liquor."

Her eyes were beginning to droop. It was about time to call her a cab. *One more question.*

"Hey, Josie. Something I don't understand. Why did your dad leave Victoria his house instead of you? It doesn't sound like Victoria needed the house or the money."

She made a noise like air rushing from a tire. "Nope. She didn't. But he said he was tired of helping me. Didn't want to be an enabler anymore. Whatever, Dad." She raised her glass to the dark sky. "Cheers. Death has a way of making things right."

CHAPTER FIFTEEN

A cold front had swept in overnight and added a distinct chill to the air. I decided to skip lunch in favor of taking Goldie for a walk down by the water. I wasn't prepared for her resistance to going near the shoreline, but I understood. Maybe in time. Though the irony of a water-Elemental owning a dog that was afraid of the water didn't go unnoticed.

We ended up at Straub Park. Goldie chased a tennis ball around for a bit while I sat on a blanket and warmed my bones in the sun. Eventually, she grew tired and flopped down beside me to stretch out in the grass. That's when my heart gave a little leap. I shaded my eyes with my hand and squinted at the person who had just come around the corner on the sidewalk across the street. *It couldn't be.* But as she made her way toward the pet boutique, looking up at the signs, her unmistakable long brown hair and easy gait left no doubt in my reeling mind. *Willow!*

"Come on, girl." I jumped up, slipping back into my flip flops, rolling the blanket up quickly and jogging through the park with Goldie. "Willow!" I was waving like a maniac as I waited for traffic to stop so I could cross. As apprehensive as I was at seeing her again, my breathing was ragged with excitement. She turned and cocked her head in my direction, then held up a tentative hand in greeting.

"What... how did you get here?" I breathed, squeezing her in a tight hug. Her long, dark hair hung down her back and I felt its familiar silkiness on my palms. I used to brush her hair for her every night growing up. She smelled like moss and primrose. My eyes filled with tears as I realized how much I had missed her.

"I drove. Well, hello, pretty girl." Willow reached down and stroked Goldie's head as she sat patiently watching us. "Who's this?"

"This is Goldie and she's a long story." I noticed Willow was wearing the bracelet I had mailed her, which kind of felt like a peace offering. I hadn't spoken to her since I left Savannah last summer. Not that I hadn't tried. It's just that my sisters hadn't really understood why I left home and were none too happy with me. "So, you drove? From Savannah?" I stared at my sister in confusion. None of us girls had learned to drive. We didn't have to, we always had a chauffeur. Momma insisted it was safer. *How much did I miss at home?* My heart ached.

Willow just shrugged a shoulder in her nonchalant way. "Yes." She turned to the boutique. "This is yours?"

"Yeah. Well, I have a partner, Sylvia. Come on, I'll introduce you. I need to get back to work anyway."

Sylvia was ringing up a customer and chatting as we entered. I unclipped Goldie's leash and led

Willow over to the table in front of the window. "Tea?"

Her eyes followed Goldie as she went to slurp some water from her bowl and then scanned the rest of the boutique. "Sure. This is nice, Darwin. Very quaint."

Sylvia finished up, and I waved her over. "Sylvia, this is my other sister, Willow." Sylvia had met Mallory already.

"Oh!" Sylvia's eyes widened in surprise as she shook Willow's hand. "So nice to meet you. Darwin, she speaks about you sisters all the time."

Willow offered me a soft smile and said, "That's good to know." Then to Sylvia, "It's nice to meet you, too."

Sylvia motioned to the table. "Well, you two sit. Visit. I had a cancellation so I can handle the customers, and Charlie will be here soon."

"Thanks, Sylvia." We settled into the seats across from each other. "So, this is a really nice surprise. Do you have luggage? How long are you staying?"

"Just a few days." She poured herself some tea. "Your letter intrigued me. I'd like to visit this Indian Burial Mound you told me about."

"Oh, okay. Sure." When I sent the bracelet, I had written to her about the Pinellas Point Mound and told her about the Pocohontas legend and the light anomalies. I never imagined in my wildest dreams it would bring her here. I was kind of disappointed she wasn't here solely to make amends, but at least she was here. "We can go tonight after I close up the boutique if you want."

She nodded. "That'd be great. I brought some sage as an offering."

"Okay, we'll go then." We sipped our tea in awkward silence. There was so much to say. I wasn't sure where to begin. *Did she want an explanation for my leaving Savannah? Her not taking my calls for months still stung. And just showing up here? Did that mean she wasn't mad anymore?* "Glad you like the bracelet. You look good. Happy."

Her soft brown eyes moved to mine. I saw nothing but love and curiosity there. I felt my body relax with relief.

"You look happy, too." She took a sip from her cup and then her mouth curved into a grin. "So, when do I get to meet this detective boyfriend Mallory told me about?"

I felt my cheeks burn. "Mallory always did love to gossip."

Willow chuckled. "And you gave her a lot to talk about during her visit."

"I'm sure." I shook my head. I could only imagine the stories Mallory went home with. "You'll meet him tomorrow night. I'm making dinner for him."

CHAPTER SIXTEEN

"**T**his is the exit." I pointed. "So, Grandma Winters taught you how to drive and bought you this car?" I eyed the futuristic green dashboard lights. "Against mom's wishes?"

Willow nodded. "I know. I was shocked, too. She just got up from the dinner table during a visit and said, 'Come on, Willow, it's time you learned how to operate a car.'"

"I wish I could have seen mom's face." I laughed.

"She nearly choked on her rhubarb pie. She tried to protest, but grandma just held up her hand and said, 'Our girls need to be independent, Joanna. Nothing wrong with them being able to get themselves around.' Much to mom's horror, she spent three weeks with us and before she left, she took me to get my license and bought me this car."

I watched her confidently change lanes to pass an old pickup truck. "I'm so jealous."

She checked the rearview mirror and then moved back into the right hand lane. "I can teach you. It's easy."

I stared at my sister's profile. She had a small smile, but I could tell she was serious. She was younger than me by almost five years, but she had always been the sensible one, the mature one. "Well, I have kind of been wanting a convertible," I said quietly. Saying it out loud, I got excited about the idea. "One of those new VW beetles. They have the coolest colors. Turn off here."

Willow glanced at me and our eyes met. "We'll do it then. Before I leave, we'll get you a license."

"Well, all right then. We'll do it." I nodded and pointed to a place for her to park on the street in front of the Mound. "Right here's good."

When we got out of the car, we were approached by two guys with flashlights. "Evening, folks." One of them politely shined it at our feet. "Don't mind us. Just making sure things stay quiet around here tonight."

"Oh. So, y'all have started patrolling again? I heard about one of your neighbors getting attacked. Aren't you afraid the shovel-wielding vandal will come back?"

He motioned to his buddy. "That's why we're not out here alone."

I wanted to ask them about the attacker possibly being a woman, but I didn't want Bernice and her friend to get in trouble for mentioning that to me. "Good idea. Well, it's real nice of ya'll to take it upon yourselves to patrol the area. Haven't seen a ghost dog tonight, have you?"

He chuckled. "No ma'am. Though, if you've come looking for spirits, Don here's wife swears a Native American visits their home. I'm sure she'd be glad to share her stories."

"I'll keep that in mind. Tonight I'm just showing the place to my sister visiting from Savannah."

"Well, you gals be careful. Don't know what kind of kook's been tearing up the place lately. Holler if you need us."

"Will do. Thanks."

We climbed the gently sloping ground up to a large oak tree. Something felt different than the last time I was here. Heavier. Though the moon shone through the oaks a bit, it seemed darker. Willow lit a sage smudge stick as an offering to the spirits. She blew the flame out gently and placed the smoking bundle of sage in a shell on the ground. The scent mingled with the smell of damp earth.

We walked around the tree and spotted the area that had been roped off. It was too dark to look for clues tonight. I followed behind Willow as she moved toward it. She stopped beside the rope and began a chant. Low, methodical utterings that sounded a lot like the recordings of American Indian chants the ghost hunters had played on the recorder. It didn't surprise me. She was obsessed with their folklore and ways of life.

She slowly lowered herself to the ground, tucked her feet beneath her and placed her palms flat against the earth. I backed up and gave her space. I was pretty sure I knew what she was attempting. Sure enough, after a few moments, I felt the ground begin to vibrate beneath my feet. *Whoa!* I backed up further and watched in stunned silence as the earth began to obey my sister.

Tiny pebbles began to roll first, then as they picked up momentum, the earth that had been disturbed and piled around the holes began to crumble and move. I watched as Willow used her earth magick to fill in the holes and seal the Mound's wounds. My mouth hung open, and I'm pretty sure I swallowed a bug. Huge improvement over watching her struggling with her lessons to line up stones.

She stood, dusted off her hands and surveyed her work. I moved to stand next to her. I could still feel the energy she had gathered surrounding the area.

"Holy heaven on a stick, girl! Someone's been practicing," I teased.

She shrugged, but I could see her eyes shining in the dim light. I was a proud sister. I threw my arm around her shoulder and squeezed. She rested her head on my shoulder for a second and then jerked her head up.

"What?" I whispered. "Did you hear something?"

"I feel... something," she whispered back.

We both listened intently as once again the local critters grew silent. A hot wind blew through, picking up our hair and warming our faces. The hair stood up on my arms. We glanced at each other.

"I think the Guardian Spirit is here." Willow reflexively looked at the earth she had just replaced. A leaf tumbled across the surface and stuck on the yellow tape.

"Would that spirit happen to be an angry black dog?" I asked.

"Guardian Spirits are often animals, but," she shook her head, "it doesn't feel angry."

She was right. I couldn't imagine whatever this energy was that crackled around us having fangs and glowing eyes. It actually felt... protective but not angry.

As quickly as it arrived, it was gone. The frogs and crickets began to sing again. The air felt cooler and lighter.

We walked back down the sloping earth in silence, toward the car.

"Maybe it only shows its fangs to those it feels are a threat to the Mound," I offered as we fastened our seat belts. "And since you helped restore it, we weren't a threat."

Willow put the car in gear, her eyes narrowing. "Which would mean that guy you told me about really did see a spirit dog?"

"Yeah. Or something."

As we drove away my cell phone rang. I smiled, a bit surprised to be hearing from him tonight. "Hey, Will."

"Hey," there was some shuffling noise and then, "I just wanted to let you know I'll be gone for a few days. I'm packing now."

"Oh?"

"I'm heading to Tampa. It's my dad. He's had a heart attack and is in ICU. "

My own heart sank. "Oh no, Will, I'm so sorry."

"Thanks, I'll call you with an update when I know more."

CHAPTER SEVENTEEN

Frankie decided to take me out to one of her favorite restaurants to cheer me up Tuesday evening, the night I was supposed to cook for Will. She and I and Willow sat at a window table overlooking the water.

"Earth to Darwin." Frankie's voice nudged me out my thoughts. "Worry isn't going to do anybody any good."

"Sorry." I sighed, moving my attention back to the menu. "What's good here?"

"Everything." She beamed. "Course, I like the filet mignon but they have some vegetarian options for you people who like to eat like rabbits. Are you a vegetarian, too, Willow?"

"No," my sister pursed her lips, "but I usually don't eat meat out because I don't know how the animals were treated. We have a local farm that's very humane we buy meat from at home."

"Technically, I'm not, either. I do eat some fish," I complained. I realized I sounded grumpy when I said it, but I couldn't help it. I was grumpy.

Frankie snorted. "And I saw Mallory devour a steak or two while she was here. You three are as different as sisters can get, aren't you?"

Willow and I glanced at each other and I finally smiled. *She had no idea.*

Willow said, "We're the same where it counts."

"I guess we all are, where it counts." Frankie nodded as the waitress brought us a bottle of red wine and filled our water glasses.

Frankie cleared her throat and raised an eyebrow at me when she caught me staring out the window again. She turned to the waitress. "Give us a few more minutes, hon."

"Of course," she said, leaving us.

"A toast." Frankie lifted her glass. "To enjoying every minute of life because you never know what's coming at you next."

We all clinked glasses. "To sisterhood," I added, suddenly grateful to have found such a good friend in Frankie. "Blood and otherwise."

The wine was delicious, smelled like dark cherries and warmed up my insides as it blazed a trail to my belly. I took a deep breath and released it slowly. "I just should've maybe offered to go with him, you think? I mean ICU's pretty serious, right?"

Willow set her glass down slowly. "And what could you have done?"

"I don't know." I shrugged. "Said the right words, held his hand, comforted him." *Used some magick to ease his anxiety.*

"I'm sure his dad's in the best of hands, sugar," Frankie said. "And if he felt it was necessary, he would have asked you to come with him."

"I could help solve Victoria's death, then he wouldn't have to rush back."

"Well, I'm putting a freeze on serious matters tonight." Frankie tapped my menu. "You need some food, wine and laughter. You can worry and feel guilty all you want tomorrow. That's an order."

I straightened my spine with a laugh. "Yes, ma'am."

After we finally ordered, we shared some girl talk and stories. Willow was totally enthralled by Frankie's homeless life before she won the lottery. She wanted to go visit Pirate City. Frankie suggested Willow accompany her on Sunday when she served the homeless breakfast at Mirror Lake.

Willow also told Frankie about our visit to the Mound and the guardian spirit she had sensed.

"Oh! You think it was the spirit dog?"

"Could have been," Willow said. "But Darwin and I didn't sense any malice, whatever it was."

"Are you psychic, Willow?" Frankie's eyes widened. "Can you feel energy from spirits? We had a really good psychic at Landon's Halloween party last year. Wasn't he great, Darwin?"

I choked on my water. The psychic in question was Zach and yeah, he was good. Too good. "Mhm," I managed.

I had to kick my sister under the table when she opened her mouth to answer Frankie's question. After throwing me a narrowed gaze, she simply said, "No."

"She's just sensitive," I offered, feeling Willow's gaze on me. I knew it bothered her I was keeping our family gifts secret in my new life. It wasn't something we had grown up doing, and mom had tried to instill in us the belief they were indeed gifts. But, I didn't see it that way. Besides, it was my life, and she needed to respect my choice whether she agreed with it or not.

"I can't imagine why someone would keep digging up the place," I said, shifting the attention off my sister. "We met some of the neighbors who are out there keeping an eye on it at night, though. Nice folks."

"I still think it's kids who haven't learned to respect history yet." Frankie broke a steaming roll in half and buttered it. "I wouldn't mess with any sacred ground, that's for sure. That's just asking for some bad juju in your life."

I was just about to answer when I noticed a familiar face a few booths down to our left. "Tara Scarpetta."

"What's that, sugar?" Frankie asked.

"Oh," I nodded toward the booth, "Tara Scarpetta's here. She's the lady who owns Blackbeard's Bountiful Treasure, the golden retriever that was Victoria and Goldie's biggest rival when... you know... before Victoria died."

Frankie pretended to rub her neck with a precious-stone-laden hand as she turned and eyed Tara. Not that she had to worry about being caught staring. Tara only had eyes for whoever was across the booth from her. "Oh yeah. I've seen her around. She's a realtor, friends with Betsy Mills. You know the gal who comes in with the three standard poodles?"

"Yeah, I know Betsy. Well, Tara is also the owner of a black BMW and the witness to Victoria's hit and run described a black car.

Coincidence? Maybe, maybe not. Will said they've got the word out to all the area body shops to see if anyone brought in a black car for front end repair recently. They're checking out her car, too."

"The police think someone would kill over a dog show rivalry?" Willow asked.

"I know, right. Frankie was just filling me in on how cutthroat the show dog world is. And Tara thinks Victoria poisoned her dog before a big show. So, revenge? Taking out the competition? Who knows what would motivate someone to kill. Especially if they weren't trying to kill Victoria, but maybe Goldie."

"Oooo, yes." Frankie nodded. "I never thought of that. Goldie could have been the target. And Tara's dog was Goldie's biggest rival?" She swallowed a sip of wine, stared thoughtfully behind her and then pushed back from the table. "I've got to use the ladies'." She winked.

I watched as she feigned surprise while passing Tara's booth and struck up a conversation with her. Tara seemed uncomfortable and struggled to hold a smile. When Frankie walked away, Tara rested her forehead on her palm for a second and then started digging through her purse. She got up alone from the table, clutching a bouquet of flowers and headed my way.

"Tara, right?" I called before she could scamper past our table. "You're Bo's owner?"

She stopped and stared at me, her face flushed. Then her eyes narrowed, and I felt a swell of heavy, dark emotion flow from her. *Anger? Embarrassment?* I couldn't tell.

"I remember you. You were with that detective at the dog show. And you had Goldie with you." She clutched her bouquet closer to her chest. "You've adopted her then?"

"Yes." I smiled up at her and rested my chin on my hand. "She's a doll. Terrible what happened to Victoria, isn't it?" I eyed her flowers and wondered if she was a fan of lilacs.

"Sure. Yes. Terrible. Guess Goldie will just be a house dog now, with that scar and all. Poor thing." Her mouth moved into a slow smile. "You girls enjoy your dinner."

"She doesn't seem like a very nice person," Willow said as we watched her leave.

I frowned. "No, she doesn't."

Frankie had an ear-to-ear grin when she sat back down.

"Okay, spill it, Frankie. What in heaven's name was that all about?"

"That, my dear Darwin, was about a certain someone having dinner with a certain male someone who is not her husband."

CHAPTER EIGHTEEN

I had just given Goldie a bone to keep her busy when Charlie came in a bit early. *Oh good. Time to do a little more digging.*

"Hey, Willow, come on. I'll take you by Big Barnie's shop before we go to lunch today." Besides my ulterior motive, I knew she'd enjoy all the artifacts he had there.

We wandered around the store for a bit. I was enjoying watching Willow go crazy over all the stuff. As we made our way to the back of the shop I overheard arguing. I hadn't seen Big Barnie since we'd been there. Was that him yelling at someone?

"You go on and browse. I'll be right back," I told Willow. I ignored her questioning glance.

There was a small hallway in the back with a door marked "restroom" and across from that another door marked "office". The yelling was coming from the cracked office door. I flattened myself against the wall and moved my ear in front of the crack.

"Don't lie to me. I followed you last night. I know what you were doing and there is only one reason you would be doing it. How..." I recognized the voice. It was Eugene. "Oh my god, it was Victoria, wasn't it?"

"Don't you dare blame Victoria," Barnie growled. "You didn't even respect her when she was alive. You damned sure better respect her now that she's not here to defend herself."

I bit my lip. *What was Barnie doing last night? Did Eugene catch him at the Mound illegally digging for artifacts? And if so, what did that have to do with Victoria?* A loud bang made me jump.

A harsh laugh and then Eugene said quietly. "Jesus, you were in love with her, weren't you?"

There was a pause and then Barnie's voice, raw with emotion. "She was an amazing person and deserved better."

Another loud bang, maybe a chair being thrown, and then Eugene's voice was right by the door. "Stay out of my way and keep your hands off of what's mine from now on."

I leaped across the hall, flung the bathroom door open and hopped inside as Eugene emerged. His face was red and an angry bruise formed a half-moon under one eye. I closed the door as he stalked out and waited a few minutes before I snuck back out into the shop.

"So, do you think Eugene could have known about the affair and killed his wife in a fit of rage?" Willow asked as we drove to lunch.

I thought about that. "I guess anything's possible. But, by their argument it sounded like Eugene had just found out about it. Otherwise, he probably would have confronted him before now."

"How do you think he found out?"

"Well, it wouldn't be a stretch to think Josie told him. After all, that's how we found out."

Willow glanced at me, confused. "Why would she do that?"

"Who knows? I have a feeling Miss Josie doesn't do a lot of thinking before she speaks."

"Her brain is probably pickled." Willow frowned. "The mess people make."

"Amen, sister."

* * *

It was after ten and I had just removed some baked treats from the oven when my cell rang. Hopping over Goldie, who was lying in the kitchen hoping I would drop something, I grabbed my phone off the counter. It was Will.

"Hey," I said, relieved to hear from him. "How's your dad?"

"Not good." I heard him blow out a long shuttering breath. "I'm on my way back though."

My heart broke for him. I could hear the worry and frustration in his voice. "Do you want to stop by when you get in?"

"No, no. It'll be late. I just needed to hear your voice."

Smiling, I removed my oven mitt and walked over to plop down on the sofa. "Glad I could be of some service. I felt so helpless."

"There's nothing you could have done. They only let immediate family into ICU and only for a short period."

My mind searched again for something I could do. I could relieve some of his worry now that I'd been practicing again, but he was still getting used to the idea that I get psychic visions from animals. My Elemental magick would most likely send him running for the door.

"Anything exciting happening there?"

"Well, are you up for a little gossip that pertains to Victoria's case?"

"Hit me." A pause. "Ouch. Sorry, bad pun."

I chuckled. "You asked for it. So, Frankie and Willow... oh, I haven't even got a chance to tell you my sister, Willow, showed up here on Monday. Drove from Savannah, which was a shock because none of us girls learned how to drive. But she does now. Anyways, we were having dinner and who is there at the restaurant but Tara Scarpetta with a man that was not her husband, according to Frankie. Oh my heavens... I just had an epiphany. What if Victoria found out Tara was having an affair? That would be some piece of information for an enemy to have over her. She could have run down Victoria in a fit of rage. Or to keep her quiet."

"Whoa, Nancy Drew." Will laughed. "Let's stick with the facts."

"Facts are just the building blocks of a story, Will. We need the whole story." *So you can solve this case and go spend time with your dad.* "We need motivation. Oh, and also something else. I overheard Big Barnie, you know that unscrupulous artifacts dealer who is supposed to be Eugene's best friend, he was yelling at Eugene. It sounded like Eugene had just found out about Barnie's affair with his wife."

"So, you were eavesdropping on a private conversation?"

"No!" I said, louder than I meant to. "If they wanted it private, they shouldn't have raised their voices and maybe shut the door all the way."

Will made some sort of noise that sounded like he was in pain. "Anything else?"

"Oh, yeah, one more thing. One of my customers told me about an attack at the Pinellas Point Mound, one of the neighbors was patrolling the Mound and got hit in the head with a shovel. Twice. He's in the hospital with a concussion."

"That's terrible, Darwin, but I don't see how that's related to the case."

I twirled a piece of bang as I thought. "I don't know. It just feels like it is somehow. I mean, Victoria was meeting Jade Harjo to give her an Indian artifact she found while cleaning out her uncle's house after he died. What if her death didn't have anything to do with someone wanting her or Goldie dead... but someone wanting that artifact? And an Indian burial ground is being vandalized, maybe because someone is illegally digging for artifacts. Just seems like too much of a coincidence. Plus, the guy who got hit with the shovel, his wife said he thought it was a woman who hit him. He's just too embarrassed to tell the police that."

"I don't know. Seems like a stretch. If the person did kill for the artifact, why did they leave it in her backpack?"

I suddenly remembered Jade Harjo's words on the Mound: *Funny thing was, your Detective Blake showed me the artifact and I don't know why she was in such a hurry to get it to me. It was just an arrowhead.*

A piece dropped into place. "What if that arrowhead in Victoria's bag wasn't the special artifact she wanted to give to Jade? Renny collected all kinds of artifacts and didn't want them sold for profit, but wanted them reunited with the Native Americans where they belonged. So, maybe she was bringing Jade the arrowhead *and* something else. Something that the killer did take from her backpack?"

"What would be important enough to kill for? It would have to be worth a lot of money. Besides, she was an unarmed woman, if someone wanted something she had, it would have been easier to just rob her. No, I think the theory about Victoria finding out about Tara's affair seems more plausible. She's already a top suspect because of the whole dog show rivalry. But then again, I'm exhausted so not sure how straight I'm thinking."

I sighed. "Sorry, guess it doesn't help I'm throwing all these theories at you with the day you've had. You know, your job is hard."

Will laughed. "I think you'd make a great detective, Darwin. But meanwhile, please stay out of trouble. I don't need to be worrying about you too right now."

The fatigue drew out his words, and I felt so desperate to do something to ease the worry I could hear in his voice. "Can you do lunch tomorrow?"

"I'll have to let you know. Seems I have some new questions for Victoria's husband."

"You're welcome," I teased. "Good night."

CHAPTER NINETEEN

I was just about to flip over the closed sign Thursday evening when Josie busted through the door and stumbled across the boutique, knocking into the treat table and falling behind the counter. Sylvia, who had just been about to pour us some tea, shot me a startled look. I flipped the sign and locked the door. We both walked over and stared down at her. She was huddled on the floor, holding her knees and mumbling to herself. Large black sunglasses hid most of her face.

"Josie?" I said calmly. "What's wrong? Are you hurt?"

She lifted her head and pulled off her glasses. Her face was ashen, her eyes bloodshot. "Check the door. Is anyone looking in here?"

We both turned our heads and stared at the door.

"No. No one's there." Was she having some kind of alcohol-induced hallucinations?

She collapsed against the counter and took in a shuddering breath. "They found me. I saw 'em. I'd know Deacon's thugs anywhere." She shoved her hands into her mussed hair and began to sob. Goldie dropped Gator and came over and nudged her elbow. Josie swiped at her nose with the back of her hand and gave Goldie a hug. "Thanks, girl."

I kneeled down in front of her while Sylvia stood with her arms crossed. Willow watched the whole thing from the tea table. "So someone named Deacon is looking for you? Why?"

"Money. Why else? Money makes the world go round. Money and pain." She snorted.

"So you owe him money?"

She cringed and dug in her bag, pulling out her flask with shaking hands. After a deep swig, she sagged and nodded. "A lot of money. Their kind of interest adds up fast and when you hit a losing streak... well, let's just say I dug my own grave."

Sylvia mumbled something in Portuguese and then touched my shoulder. When I glanced up, she flicked her chin toward the door.

"I'll be right back." I patted Josie's knee.

When we got out of earshot, Sylvia looked hard into my eyes and shook her head. "I know you like to help stray things, Darwin, but this girl is bad news. What she's talking about, owing gambling debt money, is very dangerous. Could be to the mob. They own Las Vegas. We cannot have that kind of trouble."

I pressed my lips together. "I know. You're right. I'll get her out of here."

"Josie?" I waited for her to open her eyes. "We've already closed the store. Can I give you a ride home?"

"No." She rolled her head back and forth. "They've probably been watching me. I'm sure they know I've been staying at dad's place."

"Is there somewhere else you could stay for a few days?"

She blew out a sigh. "Yeah. I guess I could go to Eugene the Bean's house. He's got a good alarm system. Guess I'll be skipping this town sooner than I wanted to. I'll need to talk to him about selling dad's house for me anyway."

*   *   *

Willow pulled up into Eugene's driveway. "Wait here," I told her.

I could feel Josie's body shaking as I helped her to the front door. She kept darting glances at the street. I rang the doorbell for her.

As we stood there waiting, I asked for her cell phone and put my number in. "Call me if you need anything."

She squeezed my hand. "Thanks for being so nice to me."

The door cracked open and a startled Eugene stood in front of us. "Josie? What are you doing here?"

He looked bad. He had tried to cover his bruised eye with a thick layer of foundation. *And what in heaven's name is he wearing?* I tried not to stare, but my gaze kept slipping back down to the black and red silk robe. I had heard of people not washing pillowcases of their deceased loved ones to hold on to their scent, but was it normal to wear their clothes? I hoped he was getting help with his grief. It seemed like he was one false step from going over the edge.

"I need a safe place to crash... just for tonight," she added when she saw him start to protest.

He held up a notebook. The one I saw on his table with stuff about CD's written on it. "I'm working on an article, Josie. It's a tight deadline. Can't you stay at your dad's place?"

"She's got some bad people looking for her, Eugene," I offered. "She needs a safe place tonight."

"Just for tonight," Josie pleaded. "I promise. Please?"

He sighed and held the door open wider.

"Thanks," I said as Josie stumbled into the house. I wanted to say more. To ask him if Victoria knew about Tara's affair. Or if she ever felt threatened by her. But I bit my tongue. Will was going to talk to him, so I needed to mind my own beeswax. I did lean in and give him an awkward hug, though. I couldn't help myself. He looked like a lost puppy. The scent of Victoria's perfume was still strong on the robe. Or maybe he sprayed in on there again to hold on to something from her. *So heartbreaking.* My eyes watered and I sniffed out a goodbye. "Make sure you set your alarm."

CHAPTER TWENTY

There was a barking match going on in Darwin's Pet Boutique. Pinky the peekapoo vs. Hershey the doberman puppy. Pinky was winning. She kept up the steady beat of yips and yaps like a seasoned pro. Will came through the door as I tried to bribe them with treats to settle their differences in a more civilized manner. The owners pulling and shushing wasn't working.

A loud, shrill whistle suddenly stopped everyone dead in their tracks. Hershey tilted his head, his mouth snapping shut as Sylvia came down the aisle clapping her hands.

"What is all this racket, my babies? No, no, no." She kneeled down between the two contenders in her gypsy skirt and waterproof apron, scratching each one under the chin as they sat and beamed at her like she was the best thing since sliced beef. The owners beamed at her as well. She took the peekapoo's leash from the owner. "You see. Much better. Come on, Pinky. Time for your spa day."

Will smiled as he stepped around the group but the smile didn't reach his eyes. I hurried to him and felt the wall of grief around him.

"What's wrong? What's happened?" I said, taking his hand.

"It's my dad." His blue eyes were bloodshot and glistened with unshed tears. "He... passed away last night."

My chest squeezed with the shock. I shook my head, which suddenly felt as heavy as a bowling ball. "No..." I grabbed him hard and pressed myself into him as if I could share the pain if I just got close enough. "I'm so sorry," I whispered through my own tears. I pulled back and looked up at him. "I'll get Willow to help out for an hour, let's go take a walk."

He shook his head. "I can't. I only have a few minutes. We got a hit on a black rental car that was turned in three days late and a local body shop that did work on that model. Hood and windshield work. The person paid cash. So, I have some interviews to do, and then I'm going to head back to Tampa to make funeral arrangements."

"I could probably take a few days off—"

"I appreciate it, Darwin, I do. But I'd rather do this alone."

Ouch. Why did that hurt so much? "Oh. Okay."

"We'll have that dinner as soon as I get back, I promise." He kissed my forehead. "I miss you."

I let a small smile I wasn't feeling cross my lips. "Sure."

* * *

The next three days moved like molasses. I tried to be the understanding girlfriend and not be upset that Will didn't want me by his side during such a devastating time in his life. He didn't need my support in this. *Well, why did he need me at all then?* Every time the hurt and confusion surfaced, I stuffed it down with a cinnamon roll. Sylvia was rubbing off on me. I also threw myself into work at the boutique, cleaning and organizing. Then at home, Willow and I baked treats and talked.

"So, your magick's gotten a lot stronger since I left." I pulled sweet potato bones out of the oven and stepped over Goldie—sprawled out in her favorite position on the kitchen floor—to place them on the counter. "How much do you practice?"

Willow thought for a long moment. "It's not really the time, but the intensity now. I finally got it. That place Grandma Winters kept telling us about. That seemingly infinite source of power. When I can tap into this, it doesn't drain me at all."

"Oh." I paused. "What Grandma Winters calls tapping into the Original Consciousness?"

"Yes. And it's amazing. There's this feeling of oneness with the creative power of the universe, of completeness. I can't even put it into words. And it doesn't totally leave you." Willow pushed the next batch she'd been stirring toward me. "Ready."

I was envious she had reached that point already. *Not her fault I had shunned my gift and stopped practicing though.* I stuck my finger in the batter and licked it. *Just right.*

"You remember you're making dog treats, right?" she asked with a grimace.

I shrugged. "Not really any difference, except the shape." I put my hand on my hip. "I've been thinking about what you said. About using magick to help ease Will's grief. You don't think it's unethical?"

Willow stared at me thoughtfully before she answered. "Remember what Grandma Winters says: We are just in tune with the elemental powers of nature which we are all a part of. There's nothing immoral or unnatural about our magick. Our brains are just wired differently."

I sighed. "Everyone has their own definition of natural, though and Will's definition most definitely does not include magick. He still isn't even comfortable with me getting information from animals."

Her shoulder moved slightly under strands of silky brown hair. "So, don't tell him. Just do it."

I stared at her. *Is she serious?* "Just use magick on him without his knowledge or consent? No, that wouldn't cause any trust issues." I flattened out the dough with more vigor than it called for. "Besides, I want to eventually be totally honest with him. That would be a big secret to carry."

"Bigger than being able to wield water magick to begin with?"

I frowned. She had a point. I thought about how sad he was. I glanced at the French doors. I could feel the Bay waters humming beyond them, giving me comfort. Water was medicine.

"He would take an aspirin if he had a headache, right?" I said softly. "So, for heartache... I could give him the medicine he needs."

Willow nodded. "And with no side effects."

I made my decision. "Yeah. Okay."

I still hadn't decided if I would tell him. I couldn't tell him beforehand, he'd never agree to it. But, when he felt better, when he realized I did it for his own happiness, then maybe he would accept it. "He's coming over for dinner when he gets back tomorrow night."

Willow nodded. "I'll make myself scarce. Maybe drive over and commune with the Mound."

"Not alone. Not with everything that's been going on there lately."

Willow shot me a look. "Now you sound like mom. I can take care of myself."

"Fine. Whatever," I said, offering Goldie a cooled treat. She dropped Gator and eagerly accepted it. "Don't come running to me if the ghost dog shows up or some wacko wielding a shovel."

* * *

I had everything cleaned up and dinner in the oven. It was time. Grabbing the rainwater I had collected, I went upstairs and entered the spare bedroom where I kept my chalice and book. The chalice had been keyed to my particular vibration and so it was important to keep it separated from other people's energy patterns.

"Stay, girl," I said to Goldie, who had followed me to the door. "I won't be long." I gave her a pet as she sat down to wait with Gator tucked in her jaws, and then closed the door behind me. Besides my tools, the room had a couch that converted into a bed, a glass coffee table and a flat screen TV mounted on the wall. I lowered myself onto my zafu cushion in front of the coffee table and poured the rainwater into the chalice. I then lit the two candles and put some rock salt into the rain water. It helped clean up any negative energy the water absorbed. I pushed the leather book to the corner of the table. I wouldn't need it for this.

First thing's first... clearing my mind. Closing my eyes, I took a deep breath in and filled my lungs, then followed the air back out. I repeated this ritual until I felt my shoulders relax and saw the empty blue sky, my symbolic image of a clear mind. Clouds of thought drifted in.

Should I really do this? Am I doing no harm? Do I really feel like this is the best thing for Will?

Yes. Let go. Yes. Let go. Yes. Let go.

I felt myself fall deeper into my own consciousness. Everything slipped away except a translucent violet light. I moved my attention there and settled into the seat of my consciousness. From here, I reached out with my energy to the water in the chalice. Immediately, I felt an expansion of power, a pulsing. I held an image of Will in my mind. When it was solid, I brought forth feelings of love and happiness for him. White hot feelings with streaks of blue and violet. I opened my eyes. The light fused with the water molecules, making them glisten like tiny prisms of glass beads.

I pulled myself back. It was done. And so much easier done with my chalice. I'd have to thank Mallory for bringing it to me, even though I *had* left it behind on purpose.

CHAPTER TWENTY-ONE

Will arrived looking exhausted, with dark half-moons under his eyes and a sallow complexion. I wrapped my arms around his neck and let him bury his face in my shoulder. We just stood like that until Goldie's panting and circling made us laugh and separate so Will could give her a proper hello.

He scratched her under her ears with both hands as her tongue lolled to the side. "I think she's actually smiling."

"Yeah, she's starting to act a little happier lately." I slipped my hand in his and led him to the table. "Come sit down. I know you haven't eaten all day."

"You know me too well." Will squeezed my hand. "Something does smell good."

"Five cheese eggplant lasagna." I called over my shoulder on the way to the kitchen. "It's my mom's recipe. Family comfort food."

"Could use some of that." Will pulled out a chair. "Speaking of family... is your sister here? Do I finally get to meet her?"

"Oh, no, sorry. She wanted to spend some time at the Pinellas Point Mound tonight," I said, as I retrieved the salad and checked the timer on the oven. "You'll meet her soon. Fifteen minutes. We'll start with this." I placed the bowl on the table as Will poured the white wine into our glasses. I glanced at his water glass. He hadn't touched it yet.

I held up my wine glass. "To the memory of your dad, who will always live in your heart."

Will's eyes deepened with sadness and a wave of grief almost made me cry out. I concentrated on steady breathing and blinking back the tears until it passed.

"Cheers." He clinked my glass and squeezed my hand.

After a sip of the citrusy wine, I spooned the salad into our bowls. "So, how was it? The funeral?"

"As good as funerals get, I suppose. He had a lot of friends. That was nice to see." I let the silence fall between us as he chewed a bite of salad in case he needed to talk more. He did, but he seemed to be talking to the salad. "The burial was hard. Brought up memories of burying my brother. And mom. They're all together now." He choked on a lump in his throat and reached for the water.

As his lips touched it, I felt a twinge of panic. *What if he reacted like Goldie did? What if I was doing something wrong?* No going back now. I grabbed my wine as his adam's apple bobbed up and down with the swallows of water.

"So," my voice squeaked. "Dinner should be about ready. Let me go check on that." I hit the table with my knee as I was getting up and winced.

"You okay?" Will asked, his eyes moving from my knee to my face.

"Yep," my voice squeaked. "Hunky dory." I limped away from the table and immediately tripped over Goldie who had taken up her position lying between me and Will. "Oh, sorry!" I felt on the verge of hysterics as she looked up at me with knowing eyes. *Don't judge me. It's for his own good.* I pursed my lips and practically ran into the kitchen and hid behind the refrigerator.

"Just be a sec," I called out. My heart was racing and the back of my neck felt damp under my hairline. *Calm down, Darwin.* I took a deep breath. This was ridiculous. All I wanted to do was help the man I loved feel better, for heaven's sake. I didn't think all this guilt would come with a good deed. I talked myself down from the ledge and removed the pan of eggplant lasagna from the oven. Plastering a smile on my face, I carried our plates to the table, being extra mindful of anything I could trip over.

"Here we go." I couldn't look at Will as I gave him his food.

"Smells really good, Darwin." I could tell he was staring at me. "You all right? You seem a little flustered."

I waved his concern off, "I'm fine," and quickly changed the subject, trying not to stare at his half-empty water glass or him for any signs of magick working. "So, how did the interviews go before you left?"

He nodded and wiped his mouth with a napkin. "The girl at the car rental company remembered the person they rented the black car to. Only because the person, a woman with dark hair and ball cap, was acting nervous and didn't remove her sunglasses."

I stopped chewing. "Do you think it was Josie?"

Will nodded. "She's definitely a person of interest. Now that it seems it wasn't just a random drunk driving incident. Especially since you'll never guess whose credit card was used to rent the car."

I made a hurry up motion with my hand. "Don't keep me in suspense."

Will chuckled. "One Miss Victoria Desoto-Roth."

My mouth dropped open. "Huh?" I shook my head. "She rented the car that ran her over?"

"Or someone stole her credit card. I had someone look into Josie and she's got an arrest record. For theft."

"I guess she does have motive, if she really wanted her dad's house." I mulled that over with a bite of food. "And the repair shop?"

"Same. Woman with dark hair, sunglasses. Paid cash there, though."

"Well, it could've also been Tara Scarpetta. She could have just as easily stolen Victoria's card at a show and she has motive... and no alibi for that night."

"True, but," Will put his fork down, turned in his seat and grabbed my hand. "Enough shop talk. I missed you." His eyes were sparkling, his face flushed as he lifted my hand to his lips and pressed a warm kiss on my knuckles. I would have enjoyed it immensely if I wasn't noticing his abrupt mood shift... upwards. *Ladies and gentlemen, we have lift-off.*

I placed my other hand on top of his. "How are you feeling?"

Will's face broke out into a grin. "I'm not hungry anymore." He pulled me up from the table. "At least, not for food," he growled as he swept me off my feet and carried me to the sofa.

Oh heavens. I couldn't reap rewards from my own deception. He held me tight in his arms, one hand palming my face as he kissed me... or rather melted me. He pressed his forehead against mine and moaned. "I feel like all the troubles in the world go away when I'm with you. How do you do that?"

I pulled back. A nervous giggle escaped my lips. That's it. I couldn't lie to him. Life would have been much easier if I could have. If I could've just enjoyed his happiness. But I couldn't live with the secret between us. "Funny you should ask that." I could hear the nervousness in my voice and I hated it. "Will, I need to tell you something."

He wrapped his fingers in mine and smiled. "Yes, you do. You need to tell me that you love me." He leaned down and kissed my forehead, my cheek, my neck. "And that I make you feel good, too."

It took every ounce of will power, and probably some borrowed from the universe, for me to not say exactly that. "Will, you know how I have that special gift?"

"With animals, yeah," he mumbled, his lips on my collarbone.

"Mmmm..." I squeezed my eyes closed. *Be strong. Do the right thing.* "There's more to it than that."

"Yeah?" He pulled back a bit, but brought my wrist with him, planting a kiss there as his eyes met mine. My heart did a funny little somersault.

"I... I also have this special gift with water. I can add properties to it to make it... medicinal. And the water you drank tonight, well, it was this medicinal water. That's why you're feeling so much better. Emotionally." I didn't dare blink as I watched his flushed face for a reaction.

His lips contorted to the side. "I don't understand. You put something in my water?"

"Yes and no." Now I wasn't sure how to explain it. "Nothing physical. It's just water. But I infused feelings of love and happiness into it. So you wouldn't feel such heavy grief. It was just hard to watch you suffer when I could do something about it."

"Oh, feelings of love," Will's mouth turned up in a seductive grin. "Okay, whatever you say, darling Darwin."

Crap on a cracker. He doesn't believe me.

"Will..." I took his face in my hands and made him look into my eyes. "I'm not joking. It's Elemental magick. It's part of... who I am."

Will's face fell, and he sat up straighter on the sofa. I let my hands fall into my lap and waited, feeling the anxiety coiling in my belly. He turned to stare out the French doors. There was only darkness beyond them, so I knew he was thinking.

Finally, he turned back to me. "If you believe you did this, I'm not sure how to feel. Because I should be angry with you for manipulating me. It's like someone giving their date ecstasy, right?"

I didn't answer. *He was kind of right but it was for a different reason. That makes a difference, right?* I was afraid to move so I just sat there and watched the confusion distort his handsome face, hoping he would come to a conclusion with a happy ending. *After all, that's all I wanted in the first place.*

"But, if it was possible for you to do this, would I even be able to feel angry at you?" He looked at me then. Right in my eyes, searching for an answer.

"I don't know," I whispered. "Will, I just wanted you to be happy."

"I was happy. With you." He dropped his head. "Grief couldn't touch that." He looked at me. "But this... this could, I think."

I started to shake my head no. He got up slowly from the couch and went to the door and turned. "Did you ever stop to think maybe I want to be sad? That this grief is the only connection to my dad I have left, and I'm not ready to let that go?"

I could only stare at him, a painful lump forming in my throat. *He was right.*

His jaw twitched. "We'll talk about this when I have a clear head, Darwin. Good night."

He was gone.

"I'm so sorry," I whispered to the empty room.

I just stood there until Goldie nudged my hand with her nose. Unable to hold back the tears, I collapsed on the floor and held onto her for dear life. She sat there patiently, letting me use her as a Kleenex until my sobs turned into hiccups. I stroked her ears. "Thanks, girl."

Then began the process of clearing our dishes from the table. I felt like a zombie as I removed all evidence of the botched evening.

Goldie started scratching at the French doors.

"If you have to go out, girl, we've gotta go out the front."

She sat down, looked back at me and whined. "All right. Chase lizards it is." I opened the doors and stepped out onto the balcony. The air was chilly and filled with fragrance from my table full of flowers. I went to the edge and gazed at the Bay beyond the park as Goldie sniffed around the table for her prey.

The sounds of traffic and music rolled beneath me. There was a rhythm to nightlife in St. Pete that I normally found comfort in. Sure, it might be a new night, different couples, a different band, but the energy was the same. Carefree, enjoying the fruits of life. Tonight, it just made me feel lonelier.

Suddenly the hairs stood up on my arms. A figure stepped out of the shadows of the park's large banyan tree and moved to the edge of the street. I froze.

Is that...? Zach? I hadn't seen him since that night at the airport. I didn't even know if he stayed at his mom's condo or left town. In fact, I made it a point not to know. If that was him, why was he standing around in the park?

Goldie nudged my leg with her nose. I glanced down. When I glanced back up, he was gone. I scanned the park and the street. Too dark. I shivered.

"Come on, girl. Let's go in."

CHAPTER TWENTY-TWO

"How'd it go?" Willow asked, coming home and peeking at the barely touched food on the kitchen counter.

"Don't ask." I sighed. "Tell me about your night. Any activity at the Mound?"

"Yeah. I met a Native American lady named Jade and her daughter, Kimi. Real nice folks. They were there performing some kind of ceremony over a new hole, just finishing up when I got there. I fixed it after they left." She grabbed a water out of the fridge and came to stretch out on the sofa.

"Yeah, I've met them there before. Jade recognized Goldie, told me Victoria was like a daughter to her, too. Did they have any ideas about who might be disturbing the place?" I made a cup of mint tea and joined her.

"No, but they did give me a little more history behind the Mound. Apparently it was a part of a large Tocobago Indian village until the Spanish explorers arrived. The balance of power shifted between the different tribes in the Tampa Bay area, depending on who the Spanish were backing at the time. Oh, and by the wealth of treasures they were scavenging from the Spanish shipwrecks. Eventually they were defeated by the Spanish attacks and the new infectious diseases the Spanish brought with them."

"Sad," I said.

"Yeah. It's nice the remaining people of the tribe still hold on to their heritage. They still hold the same things sacred as their ancestors; keep their culture and beliefs alive. That is true immortality."

"Cultural immortality?" I mused.

"I suppose." Willow stared at me. "So, you really don't want to talk about it?"

I groaned. "Let's just say Will did not jump up and down and thank me when I told him what I did."

"Why did you have to tell him? Mallory said he has a closed mind, so did you really think he would understand?"

My first reaction was to be mad at Mallory. But, I let that go because she was right. Will did have a closed mind, but it wasn't his fault. That's just how he's built. He believes in facts, things he can see, touch and prove. That's also what makes him a great detective. I closed my eyes. "I know. I know." I rubbed my forehead between my eyes. "I think I'm going to hit the sack. Tomorrow's a new day, right?"

"Always," Willow said softly.

That night, Goldie and I were both restless. She kept rising and circling the bed until she finally hopped down and stretched out on the floor. I was probably bothering her with all my flailing human limbs and sheet-wrestling matches (which I lost).

Eventually, I fell into a fitful sleep. That's when "the dream" happened.

The air shimmered around me like a desert mirage. Sugary sand warmed my bare feet, water circled me. Large white caps rose beyond the sandy shore, moving toward me and crashing at my feet. They lulled me, and I felt my body swaying as if responding to some beat I couldn't hear. What I could hear, over and above the crashing sea, was a rumbling. I could also feel it beneath the sand. I squinted through the gauzy air toward the looming mountain, gaining more detail as I stared. Like a sudden fireworks display, fluorescent red spewed from the mountain, igniting the air.

I took a few steps back and stumbled, landing with a soft thunk in the sand. A figure began to shimmer and solidify in front of me. I gasped. *Zach*.

He reached down and held out his hand. I stared into the depths of his dark eyes as I placed my hand in his, feeling the familiar sensation of heat spread through my body. He pulled me up to stand before him, releasing my hand but instead of letting me go, he slid it to my waist and pulled me closer. My hand went to his bare chest and laid there still. A soft gasp escaped my lips. I glanced down at the tattoo on his chest and felt the sudden need to trace it. As my finger moved around the symbols, down toward where his pants hung low on his waist, he moaned. The symbols changed from black to fluorescent red. The same color as the lava shooting through the air behind us.

"Darwin." He whispered my name and it echoed all around us. His index finger tilted my chin up to meet his eyes once again. His mouth came down softly to touch mine. Heat spread to my core as he deepened the kiss. Lost. I was lost in him. Lost to him. His arm tightened around me, pressing me against his chest until I felt nothing but pressure, heat and passion. His grip, his kiss, his dark, hungry eyes clearly said "mine".

I tore my mouth from his with effort that almost made me black out. "No." I breathed. I watched his glistening lips turn up in a half smile.

He nodded. "In time."

I flailed in the bed, trying to untangle myself from the sheets and fell off the side of the bed in the process. Goldie lifted her head at the loud thunk.

I lay there, staring at the ceiling, breathing like I had just run a marathon. Pressing my hand to my chest, I could feel the heat radiating off my body as if I'd been lying out in the sun. I reached a hand up and pressed my lips. Hot. I shivered.

I replayed his words over, "In time." What did that mean, in time? *Gah!* I pushed myself off the floor. *It was just a dream, Darwin. Your psyche is punishing you for hurting Will. You didn't actually cheat on him with Mr. Dark and Dangerous. Just. A. Dream.*

CHAPTER TWENTY-THREE

Despite the constant stream of customers at the boutique, the day dragged.

"Darwin? You feeling okay?" I glanced up from the computer screen. Willow stared at me, her expression somewhere between amused and sympathetic.

"Yeah. Just a bunch on my mind." *Like Will not calling me today. And like a dream so real, I was feeling all kinds of guilt about it.* "What's up?"

Her expression changed to one of excitement. "I'm going to have dinner tonight with Kimi. She's got some artifacts to show me. Do you want to come?"

"Oh, I don't want to be a third wheel." I waved her off. "You go on."

"You wouldn't be a third wheel, and besides, what are you going to do? Sit upstairs and eat leftovers by yourself and wait for the phone to ring?" She crossed her arms. "I can't let you do that. It's too pathetic."

"Your sister is right," Sylvia threw at me as she walked by. "Go out."

"I'm feeling a little ganged up on," I mumbled. Willow was still staring at me with that look I knew all too well. Her stubborn one. "All right, fine. I'll go."

We were meeting at Coconuts, a pet-friendly restaurant, so I brought Goldie with me. I said it was so she didn't have to be alone, but the truth was, I was getting pretty attached to her. She was a calming presence in an otherwise rocky few weeks.

"Hi!" Kimi waved as we approached the outdoor table. Thankfully, her mom and the gray-haired gentleman from the Mound were with her. I smiled in relief. I didn't feel so awkward tagging along.

We greeted each other and Goldie got pats all around as we sat down.

Jade said, "This is my friend, Sal White."

"Nice to meet you Sal." I smiled. "I saw you at the Mound. Y'all are part of the Spirit People, right? What exactly is it your group does?"

"We're just a small part of a larger intertribal group," Jade answered. "Our main goal is to keep our ancestors' memories and beliefs alive. We believe they fought and died for things that shouldn't be just buried with them."

"I see. Thanks," I said as the waitress poured us all water.

"They like to protest things, too," Kimi grinned at her elderly mother. "Like the poor non-Native American woman charging for sage smudging and calling herself Eagle Cloud. I thought she was going to have a stroke when you told her she was stealing and abusing your culture."

"Well, she was," Sal said simply.

"Forgive my ignorance, y'all," I said, "but why does it bother you when non-Native Americans practice your traditions? They say imitation is the highest form of flattery."

"Yes." Jade sighed. "We realize it's a hard thing to understand. But, these ceremonies, the way we dress, are part of our religion. We don't want them exploited as entertainment or for profit."

"My mother used to say it was like charging people for a baptism," Sal offered.

"Oh, I see." I nodded.

"That is also why we don't like our artifacts sold for profit. We collect as many as we can and donate them to the museum," Jade said. "That way our culture stays alive, people learn about it, but it's not exploited."

"Which reminds me." Kimi pulled an item wrapped in tissue paper from her bag slung over the chair. "This is the human effigy urn I was telling you about." She unwrapped it and held it out to Willow.

"Oh wow," Willow whispered, taking the clay vessel carefully into her palm and eyeing it with wonder. "Look at the detail in the figure. You can even tell his eyes are closed. You said a woman had this for fifty years?"

"Yes, she recently passed and her son gave it to us."

I frowned. "You know, Jade, I was thinking about what you told me about the arrowhead in Victoria's bag. Do you think it's possible there was a second artifact and the person did in fact take it when they went through her bag?"

Jade's head jerked up and her eyes widened. "I hadn't thought of that." She glanced at Kimi and they shared a questioning look. "She was so sure I was going to be surprised. Maybe it was something that would have been valuable and whoever saw it recognized that."

"He sure owed us more than an arrowhead," Kimi mumbled.

Jade held up her hand and shook her head slightly. Kimi folded her arms and averted her gaze.

Okay, what was that about? Why does Kimi think Renny owed them something? I glanced at Willow. Maybe she could get Kimi to open up about that remark later.

"So, Josie gets Renny's house after all?" Kimi glared at her mother. "Figures."

I felt a wave of anger emanate from Kimi. "You aren't too fond of Josie, I take it?"

"Not much to be fond of," Kimi scoffed. "She's an alcoholic, a thief, and a habitual liar with a gambling problem."

"That's enough, Kimi," Jade warned. "She's also like family."

I felt like I needed to break up the tension. "Well, if it'll make you feel better, I think she's planning on selling it... the house. And I think she's in a lot of trouble. She was hiding from some men who came from Vegas and she was real scared. I took her to Eugene's house, though he didn't seem too happy to see her."

Kimi shook her head. "I can't imagine why." The sarcasm was palpable. "I'm surprised she didn't ask you to take her to Big Barnie's place. Would've been a good excuse for her to play damsel in distress."

"Why Big Barnie's?"

"She's been in love with him for years. He doesn't want anything to do with her, though. Told her as much every time she tries to throw herself at him."

I frowned. "Well, that's stranger than a cat with two tails. She told me Victoria was the one in love with Big Barnie. Why would she say that?"

Kimi laughed harshly. "Cause she's a pathological liar, like I said." She glanced down fondly at Goldie. "Goldie was the love of Victoria's life."

Okay, I was really confused now. Did this mean Victoria and Barnie weren't having an affair? *Then what were Eugene and Barnie fighting about?*

CHAPTER TWENTY-FOUR

We exited the restaurant, and I left a message for Will, telling him what I'd found out about Josie. I wished he had answered so I could find out if he asked Josie about Victoria's credit card yet. But apparently he still wasn't talking to me. I noticed I had a missed call and a message. Odd. I didn't recognize the number.

I listened to the message once, then shook my head and put in on speaker. "Willow, listen to this."

"Darwin? Hey, It's Josie..." I turned up the volume because she was whispering. "Oh my god, girl! I've found something. My crazy old dad wasn't so crazy after all. Meet me at Big Barnie's house, 1465 S. Banyan Street—"

There was a thump like the phone was dropped and then nothing. Disconnected.

I peeked around Goldie, who had her head between us, panting up a storm. "What do you think that was all about?"

"Nothing good. How do we get to Banyan Street?"

I pulled up the address on my phone, my gut twisting. I had a really bad feeling about this. I tried to call Josie back on the number she called me from, but it went straight to voicemail. "Take a right here."

We parked in front of his mailbox. Eyeing the older ranch-style house, with one porch light burning, I hesitated. "Should I just knock?"

Willow shrugged. "I guess."

I nodded and opened the car door. Goldie jumped into the front seat and out the door.

"Goldie," I grumbled as I watched her squat in his front yard. Guess that was my fault for being so focused on Josie's message and not giving her a potty break after the restaurant. I walked up the driveway and Goldie trotted over to follow me.

The front blinds were pulled shut. A fat green frog watched me from his perch under the porch light as I knocked. No answer. I rang the doorbell. Waited. Nothing. I patted Goldie on the head, frowning. *Where are they?*

As we made our way back down the driveway, Goldie suddenly stopped. She lifted her nose in the air, her tail stiff behind her. And then she put her nose to the ground and took off around the side of the house.

"Goldie!" I rushed after her, hearing Willow call my name and her car door slam.

I stopped dead in my tracks, my heart leaping into my throat. "Josie?" My voice squeaked.

Willow came up behind me. I heard her sharp intake of breath. "Is she..."

"I think so," I whispered. The back porch was a cement slab with two beat-up lawn chairs. Lying very still in one of those chairs was Josie. Her eyes were open, staring. Goldie nudged her hand. "We should probably check anyway, to be sure." My eyes stung as I forced my legs to carry me over to her. I pressed two fingers to her neck. Cold. No pulse. I glanced over her unnaturally still body and started shaking. "What happened to you? Who did this?" Her bag was lying on the ground. I carefully searched through the empty liquor bottles and makeup. Whatever she had found wasn't here. *Did someone take it?*

"Let's go back to the car and call Will."

Will didn't answer his phone. I left a message and called 911. He must have checked the message because he called me right back for the address. "Be there in ten minutes. Stay in the car and lock the doors."

His tone was cold, impersonal. The tears rolled down my face. I was beginning to think maybe he wasn't just angry and waiting to cool off. What if we were over? I thumbed the ring he had given me. Willow reached over and took my hand, squeezing it. I heard her sniffle and glanced over. She was wiping at the tears on her own cheeks. I squeezed her hand back, realizing this was the first time she'd ever seen a dead body. Such a shocking moment. "I'm sorry you had to see that."

"It's okay. I'm glad I'm here with you." She closed her eyes and leaned her head back on the seat. "What do you think happened to her?"

"I don't know. Maybe Big Barnie finally got sick of her throwing herself at him. Or the thugs from Vegas found her here. There's no blood that I could see, but I guess they could've done something else to her." I glanced around the yard nervously. "Or maybe it wasn't murder. Maybe her liver just gave out or something."

"But she said she found something. And now she's... dead," Willow said quietly. "Whatever happened, I hope she didn't suffer."

"Me too." I thought about Josie's message. What did she mean her dad wasn't crazy after all? Did she find something in his house? And why did she want to meet here? Did whatever she found have something to do with Big Barnie? More questions and not enough answers.

A fire truck arrived first. We got out of the car and greeted the EMT's who jumped out.

"Back here."

We led them around the side of the house to the back where Josie was still in the same position. I was kind of hoping she would be sitting up, and we would all laugh at how we thought she was dead.

The slim, red headed EMT searched for a pulse and shook his head at his partner. They pulled out some kind of device and starting putting it on her body. As they worked, I saw more flashing lights pulsing off the house and heard more car doors slam.

Will came around the corner with four uniformed officers behind him.

"The owner doesn't appear to be home," I heard one of them say.

His eyes found mine immediately. No greeting. He turned and gave his full attention to Josie.

Moving carefully and purposefully, he surveyed the scene, instructing the officer with the camera in a low voice.

It wasn't enough I could feel the waves of hurt coming from him. It was also plain as day in his eyes when he finally did approached me.

"Let's talk over here." He motioned me to the side, away from a direct view of Josie. As he pulled out his notepad and rubbed the back of his neck, I had to fight back the tears. I knew finding me with yet another victim was not making him happy right now. Add this to our already strained relationship, and I didn't see how we would survive.

"Okay. Start from the beginning." His jaw was set hard as he looked up at me, frustration darkening his eyes.

"I wasn't trying to investigate anything, Will." I crossed my arms, trying to stop my body from shaking. "Honest. Josie came into the boutique the other night, scared out of her mind because she was being followed by some thugs she recognized from Vegas. Apparently she owed some money to a guy named Deacon." I inhaled a deep, shaky breath. "We took her over to stay with Eugene that night because she didn't feel safe staying at her father's house. She thought the thugs knew she'd been staying there." I moved my gaze from his hand scribbling in the notebook to his face, fighting the urge to smooth the wrinkles in his forehead. "Then tonight, she left me a message to meet her here." I pulled my phone out of my pocket and played the message for him. As he listened, I glanced over at Willow, who was talking to another officer. She had her head bowed. I felt bad she had to go through this.

"Do you know why she would want to meet at this specific residence?"

"No. Well, maybe. We had dinner with Jade Harjo and her daughter Kimi tonight. Kimi mentioned Josie had always been in love with Big Barnie, which surprised the heck out of me because Josie told me it was Victoria who was in love with him..." I caught Will's raised eyebrow. *Right just the facts, not town gossip.* "Anyway, this is his house. Maybe she wanted to show him whatever she found. But there was no answer when we got here, and we were about to leave when Goldie ran around the side of the house and found Josie like... that." Goldie leaned hard against my leg. I reached down and rubbed her ear. "What do you think happened to her?"

"Don't know yet. All right. You can go home now. I'll call you if there are any more questions." He shut his notebook with a smack.

I couldn't take it anymore. I touched his arm. "Will?" He looked at me without a response. "Is that the only reason you'll call me?" I heard my voice break.

He glanced down at the ground and then back up at me. "We'll talk, Darwin. I just need some time." His eyes softened but there was no smile. "Go on home."

Willow and I were silent on the drive back home, both of us trying to process the events of the night. I had so many emotions to sort through, I couldn't even think straight. I was slowly realizing underneath the sadness was anger. Anger at whoever took Josie's life and anger at the way Will was just shutting me out. I didn't feel like me trying to alleviate his grief warranted such a strong reaction. Then it hit me, he wasn't reacting just to that one action. It was me. My gifts. He wasn't comfortable with them. At all. *Could he ever be?* That was the real question.

CHAPTER TWENTY-FIVE

The next morning, Frankie showed up with the paper a half hour before we opened. This was becoming her routine when something major happened in St. Pete. She didn't really seem all that surprised when I told her I already knew about Josie's death because Willow and I had been the ones who found her. I briefly wondered what this said about my growing reputation for being in the middle of trouble.

I broke off a piece of the lemon cake she'd brought and shared it with Goldie while Frankie read the article to me and Willow. Goldie licked her lips and slapped her paw up on my knee for more.

"Local artifact shop owner and St. Pete native, Barnabus Imbach, was held for questioning in the death of Josie Desoto. Mr. Imbach said he was out for a drive and didn't know Miss Desoto was at his residence. A source stated he could not verify his whereabouts."

"He must have come home after we left last night," I said to Willow. She sipped her tea and nodded.

"Miss Desoto's body was discovered on the back porch of Mr. Imbach's residence on Banyan Street by unknown persons." Frankie stopped and grinned at me. "Hey, Will managed to keep your name out of it this time."

"Small comfort," I said. "So, Big Barnie was just driving around? That sounds a bit fishy. Does it say anything about how she died?"

"No, just that it's an ongoing investigation." Frankie paused to take a bite of her cake.

I shook my head. "Well, if she was the one who killed Victoria, I guess that investigation is closed."

"Was she a suspect?" Frankie asked, surprised.

"Yeah. Turns out a black rental car was used to run Victoria down and the credit card used to rent it was in Victoria's name. Josie would've had access to her credit cards and she had a record for theft. Plus she had motive. Victoria told her she would leave her dad's house to her in her will."

"And she needed the money." Frankie shook her head. "She was a messed up soul, but I still wouldn't have pegged her for a killer."

"Desperate times and all that," I said. Though Frankie was right. Maybe she was just so drunk, she didn't really know what she was doing. "Anyway, the other suspect high on the list is Tara Scarpetta."

"The dog show rival we saw at the restaurant?" Willow asked.

"Yeah. She had motive. Besides being rivals, Victoria could have discovered Tara's extra-marital activities."

"But, how would Tara get a hold of Victoria's credit card?" Frankie asked.

I shrugged. "She could have taken it out of her bag at a show, I guess."

"That would have to be premeditated. Not just a random act of anger. Why would she do it?"

I thought about that as I sipped my tea and checked the clock. "Maybe Victoria was blackmailing her with the information. She didn't need the money, but she did want Goldie to be the first golden retriever to win the Westminster Dog Show. Tara and Bo were obstacles to that dream."

"Hm. Okay let's go back to Josie. Say she was the one who ran down Victoria." Frankie licked her fingers and frowned. "Then who killed Josie?"

"If someone did kill her, it could have been the Vegas thugs she was hiding from."

"You don't think it was actually Big Barnie, even though she was dead on his back porch?"

I shrugged. "If he did do it, wouldn't he move the body so he wouldn't be implicated?"

"Or," Frankie said, "he would leave and pretend like he wasn't home when it happened."

"Is it always this exciting in St. Pete?" Willow frowned at me, emphasizing the word "exciting".

I knew between the stories Mallory went home with and what she had gone through in her short stay here, she was probably getting really worried about my safety. Luckily, Sylvia came in at that point and interrupted my answer.

* * *

That evening I couldn't sleep. Again.

"Hey, what are you doing up?" Willow asked.

"Just brushing Goldie. I think the fur balls lining the walls were starting to mate."

Willow came around and sat on the sofa, her arms crossed. "Couldn't sleep, huh?"

"No." I sighed, running the Furminator over Goldie's stretched out body for the millionth time. She glanced up at Willow, rolled over to give me better access to her tummy and sneezed. "Bless you."

"Want to talk about it?"

Did I want to talk about what? The fact that every time I fell asleep now, Zach was waiting there for me with those smoldering dark eyes and touch that consumed me like fire? No. Definitely did not want to talk about that. Did I want to talk about finding Josie tonight? No, not really. Will? I sighed and uncrossed my stiff legs, stretching them out on the wood floor. Yeah, maybe. Goldie rolled over and pushed herself up to get some love from Willow.

"I don't know."

"Look, Darwin, I'm sorry I was mad at you when you left home. Well, not really mad as much as hurt. But, I'm here now. Let me make it up to you."

I glanced up at Willow. How could I refuse an olive branch like that?

"It's just the more I think about Will being mad at me, the angrier I get. He's making me feel like the people in Savannah did, you know? This is why I came here and didn't want anyone to know about our family. I was tired of being judged, of feeling bad about myself because of what other people said about us. And here I go again. I open up to one person, who supposedly loves me, and I'm right back in the same place. Judged and feeling bad about myself."

Willow stroked Goldie's ears. "Will seems like a nice guy, Darwin, but he's the first guy you've dated. Maybe he's not the right one for you. Love means acceptance and if he can't accept who you are—"

"I know," I interrupted. "But, say I date someone else. Eventually, I'd have to expose myself to them, too. Then wait to see if they rejected me. I can't even imagine going through this again." I groaned. "Plus I don't want to. I really do love Will. When I think about not having him in my life, my heart physically hurts."

"Guess everyone can't be as lucky as dad. Mom accepted him without question."

"She was seventeen. We accept everything without question at that age. We're not jaded yet."

CHAPTER TWENTY-SIX

Checking the clock again, I sighed. The day was going about as fast as a herd of turtles. Willow and Sylvia kept trying to cheer me up with food. I just wanted to go home and immerse myself in a big old tub full of water until I was a prune. But I had one thing to do before that.

As we locked up, I turned to Willow. "Mind driving me over to Eugene's house? I need to at least offer to help with any arrangements he needs to make with Josie. He hasn't even gotten over his wife's death yet and now he has to deal with another funeral."

"Yeah, sure." She grabbed Goldie's leash as I locked the door. "I wanted to check on the Mound tonight anyway, before it gets dark. We can swing by Eugene's house after that."

As we pulled around the corner onto Mound Place, we spotted a patrol car parked by the entrance. Two officers were just exiting the wooden fence barrier. I recognized the young, lanky one from the pirate ship wedding.

"Hey." I waved, as we got out the car. "Officer Starks right? We met at Mike Mann's wedding on the pirate ship."

He pointed at me with a nod. "Oh yeah, Detective Blake's girlfriend. Darwin, right? Couldn't forget a name like that."

Girlfriend. I forced out a quiet, "yeah," and nodded toward the Mound. "So, what's going on? More trouble?"

"More vandalism last night. I wouldn't be out here if I were you girls. We're going to start patrols around the area."

"Any theories?"

"Probably just unsupervised teenagers with nothing better to do. But since a neighbor was assaulted, we're taking the vandalism more seriously."

"Mind if we take a look? We'll be quick."

"Go ahead. It's still open to the public for now. Like I said, though, you're taking a risk being here at night."

"Thanks, Officer Starks."

I nodded at Willow as the patrol car eased away, knowing she wanted to fix whatever the vandals did. "Go ahead. I'll take Goldie for a little walk."

The stars were out. Goldie happily sniffed the grass along the side of the street. It would be a perfect evening if not for the questions bumping around in my head.

Willow looked tired when she slid back into the car. She sighed.

"How bad was it?"

"It was a pretty deep hole. I fixed it, but left the police tape so Jade and Kimi could bless the ground. Your theory about someone looking for artifacts does seem more and more plausible every time one of these holes shows up."

"Yeah, except there's nothing there. Remember what Veronica said? Archeologists have been all over it. There was nothing but some shell tools found."

Willow gave the Mound one last glance before pulling away. "Maybe someone buried something there recently?"

"And what? Forgot where they buried it?" I let my head fall back against the seat and closed my eyes. "Well, let's just hope the police patrols can put a stop to it. Whatever or whoever is buried there deserves some peace."

I must have dozed off because before I knew it, we were pulling into Eugene's driveway. Goldie started whining. I picked Gator up off the backseat and gave it to her for comfort. "Stay here, girl. It's okay."

There were no outside lights on, but I could see lights on inside through the beveled-glass windowpane that ran the length of the door. As I approached, movement caught my eye. Through the window, I could see someone walking up the stairs. I squinted through the glass at the distorted image. Was that...?

A woman with long, dark hair was climbing the stairs. My heart sped up. I flattened myself against the door in case Eugene was close by and peered back through the window. Was that Kimi? Was she wearing Victoria's robe? Curse the beveled glass.

I squat-ran back to the car and slid in. "Go, go, go," I whispered.

"What's wrong?" Willow quickly backed out of the driveway.

"I don't want Eugene to know that I know," I whispered, staring at the house to make sure he wasn't coming out the door.

"You're not making any sense," Willow said, adjusting her rearview mirror.

"None of this makes any sense." I sat up in the seat and clicked my seatbelt in place. "There was a woman in there with long, dark hair. I think she was wearing Victoria's robe. That is just so wrong." I didn't mention the woman looked like Kimi. Willow was really fond of her and what if I was wrong?

Willow took in that information. "So, Eugene has a girlfriend already? He didn't really seem in the dating frame of mind."

"No, he didn't. It's a bit soon for a woman to be walking around the house like she owns the place, don't you think? What if he was having an affair while Victoria was alive? And don't you think it's strange the witnesses said it was a woman with long, dark hair who hit Victoria and now such a woman is in her house?"

"You think it's his mistress and she killed Victoria?"

"I don't know." I took out my phone and called Will. "What I do know is we now have another dark-haired woman to add to the suspect list." Of course, the main evidence was the black rental car and the fact someone used Victoria's credit card to rent it. Which means they would have had to have access to her things. Being in her house would definitely give this new suspect access. And if it was Kimi, she would've known her mother was meeting Victoria that night.

I rolled my eyes. "Of course, he's not picking up," I mumbled and left a message.

CHAPTER TWENTY-SEVEN

I decided I needed to throw a dinner party. It would be a great distraction to get my mind off of Will and a good excuse to invite Kimi over. I planned on bringing up the fact Eugene might already be seeing someone to see how she reacted. Would she be embarrassed? Jealous? I'd find out tonight. Besides, if nothing came of it, Willow was thrilled with the idea of spending time with her and Jade.

"Mmm, that smells amazing!" I hurried down the stairs with my hair still wet from the quick shower. "You always were the best cook."

"Thanks." Willow grinned, her face flushed from the warm kitchen. "I still have to cook the stuffed mushrooms. How long do we have?"

"About an hour." I pulled out a can of Goldie's food. She began turning circles in the kitchen and let out a small *woof!* "I'm hurrying," I said. "Someone's appetite is back in full force. Must be all the yummy smells in here."

Willow plucked the can from my hand. "You go finish getting ready. I've got everything covered here."

"Thanks, Sis. It's really great to have you here." I gave Willow a quick hug and she shooed me from the kitchen.

* * *

Frankie showed up first, toting Itty and Bitty in a green designer bag that matched her outfit; her boyfriend, Jack, by her side.

"Hey, y'all. You look fabulous, as always, Frankie." I gave her and Jack a quick hug. "Come on in."

"Thanks for the invite, Darwin," Jack said. "Nice to see you."

"You, too. Been awhile." I motioned to the basketful of wine bottles on Jack's arm and laughed. "Looks like y'all raided someone's wine cellar."

"What?" Frankie chuckled. "You did say this was a party? And oh my good gracious, what is that delicious smell?" She shuffled into the kitchen where Willow had just removed the stuffed mushrooms from the oven.

"That's the *dinner* part of the dinner party." I shook my head as I showed Jack where to put his offering.

Sylvia and Landon arrived next with a bakery box I didn't even dare open. Jade and Kimi also arrived with some of their own delicious smelling offerings. As laughter and conversation filled the townhouse, I was trying really hard not to think about the fact that Will should be here. And the fact that he hadn't even talked to me in four days.

How could I feel alone with all these happy souls around me? *Stop feeling sorry for yourself, Darwin. Be grateful for the wonderful people who are here.*

"Oh, just squeeze it in anywhere there's room," I said to Jade, who was eyeing the table for some place to unload her food.

"Okay, I think there's a spot right there." She pushed aside a plate of deviled eggs. "Perfect. Oh, hey, sweetheart." Jade reached down and scratched Goldie, who had trotted over and sat in front of her, her tail swishing the floor. "Yes, I brought you a treat. You must smell it, smarty girl." Goldie inhaled whatever Jade gave her and licked her chops, eyes locked on her pocket hopefully. "Oh, and who do we have here?" Jade asked as Itty and Bitty came over to see if there were any more handouts. "Aren't you two just precious?" She squatted to give them some scratches under their dainty chins.

"Those are Frankie's dogs, Itty and Bitty," I offered. "They'll mooch off you all night if you let them."

"Sorry I don't have any more treats. I'll sneak you two something later. Don't tell your mom."

"You need a dog, Mom." Kimi walked over shaking her head. "Where do you want the frybread for the chili, Darwin?"

"Just squeeze it in anywhere." I rearranged the cheese and veggies to try and give her some room. "Wow, lots of amazing food here. I hope everyone's hungry."

"*Estou!* I could eat a horse." Sylvia pulled Landon over to the table. "Smells *delicioso.*"

"You don't count," I teased. "You're always hungry."

"I don't know where she puts it." Landon wrapped his arm around her waist and buried his nose in her neck.

She tilted her head to whisper something to him and they both laughed. My heart ached a little. *Stop it, Darwin.* You've been alone for twenty-eight years and are fine. I sighed. *Yeah, but now I knew what I was missing. And that was Will.*

I busied myself lighting the candles on the kitchen bar and dining table and putting on some background music while Jack played bartender.

Frankie caught up with me and handed me a glass of something white and cold. "So, have you heard the news?" She glanced around. "Where's Will anyway?"

"We're kind of having a thing... a fight I guess." I waved that thought off. "Long story. What news?"

"They arrested Tara Scarpetta." She took a sip of her wine and nodded at my open mouth. "Crazy, right?"

"For Victoria's murder?" I asked when I could speak.

"Yes! Betsy Mills called me. She was with Tara at the real estate office when they showed up to arrest her. Apparently a witness from the night Victoria died identified her in a photo lineup, though he wasn't one hundred percent positive because he was on his boat. But then, another witness from the car rental place picked her out of the photo lineup, too. And she couldn't give them her whereabouts that night so they brought her in."

"What's going on?" Willow asked as she brought some silverware and napkins to the table and saw my face.

"Tara Scarpetta, Victoria's dog show rival, has been arrested for her murder."

Willow looked from me to Frankie. "I guess that's good, right? That they've solved her death."

"Yeah, it's good," I said, still digesting the news and everything it meant. Did all the pieces fit? I couldn't think.

"I can't believe it," Frankie said. "You just never really know about people."

"Yeah." I answered, still thinking about the implications of Tara being the killer. Did she do it on purpose? Did she just mean to knock Goldie out of the competition or did she actually mean to kill Victoria? "I guess the police can concentrate on finding out who killed Josie now."

Frankie motioned to me and Willow. "It must have been such a shock for you girls, finding her dead like that."

"*You* found her?" Kimi asked, as she and her mom joined the conversation.

I sipped my wine and nodded. "Yep, with Goldie's help."

Kimi's dark eyes were hard to read as she asked, "How?"

"Josie had left a message on my phone. I got it right after we went to dinner with y'all that night. She said she found something, and her dad wasn't crazy after all."

Jade and Kimi stared at each other, their eyes widening.

I watched them curiously. "Anyway, she said she was going to Big Barnie's house and wanted us to meet her there. I'm thinking she found something, an artifact maybe? An artifact that proved his Gasparilla story was true. What do y'all think?" Actually, that idea just popped in my head. But, that was the only thing I knew of that made people think he was a little off his rocker.

Kimi shook her head slightly at her mom, but Jade ignored her. "Maybe she found the treasure map."

"Treasure map?" We all said at the same time.

"Yeah, Renny used to tell a story about an engraved copper map that was passed down from his great-great-grandfather, the one who supposedly pirated with Gasparilla," Jade replied. "Said it told the coordinates of a treasure buried right here in St. Pete. Part of the spoils his crew— including Renny's ancestor—took off with after Gasparilla was taken down by a U.S. Navy warship."

"That's quite a story. Did anyone ever see this map?" I asked.

"Nope."

I eyed Jade. I couldn't tell if she believed it or not. "Okay, for the sake of argument, say a map did exist and Josie found it. Why would she take it to Big Barnie?"

"Barnie would be her best bet if she wanted to figure out the map," Jade said. "Plus, like Kimi said, she's been in love with him forever. Eugene and

Barnie used to eat up Renny's stories as kids and always dreamed of finding the treasure one day. They always believed him."

"Of course," Frankie said. "A story like that is tailor made for little boys."

I looked at Frankie thoughtfully. "True and there's still nothing to prove it exists. Josie didn't have a map on her when we found her. I checked her bag before the police got there." I shook my head. "And if it did exist, why didn't Renny try to find the treasure himself?"

Kimi and Jade both nodded. "That was the million dollar question. And the reason we believe it was just a story he liked to tell."

But if it did exist, it was a good motive for someone to kill Josie.

"All right," Frankie said as Jack came over and freshened up her drink. "I'm trading in pirates for magicians. Landon looks like he's putting on quite a show over there."

"Cool!" Kimi said.

I held up my hands. "Please fill your plates first or y'all are going home with leftovers."

As everyone obligingly filled their plates and began migrating into the living room, something was still bothering me. I needed to know the identity of the mystery woman in Eugene's house.

"Hey, Kimi?" I stopped her before she joined the others. "Can I ask you something?"

"Sure."

"How well do you know Eugene?"

"Pretty well, why?"

"I think Eugene is seeing someone already. Would that surprise you?"

Kimi blinked and kept her expression neutral. "Not really. People deal with grief in many different ways."

I wanted to ask if she had any idea who he might be seeing and also, why she made that comment about Renny owing her something, but Sylvia interrupted.

"Darwin!" She threw Kimi an apologetic look. "Sorry, sorry, I just cannot wait. I'm so excited to ask you if you will be my maid of honor?"

My hand went to my heart, Eugene and his mistress forgotten. "Of course!" I'd never been asked to be a maid of honor and was surprised at how touched I felt. It truly did feel like an honor.

"*Muito obrigada*." Sylvia grinned, squeezing me in a one-armed hug while balancing her plate in the other hand. "You will help me plan then. There's so much to worry about, flowers and cake and invitations."

I nodded, flushed with excitement. "Don't worry. We have lots of time and it'll be fun." I noticed Kimi had taken the opportunity to slip away. Sylvia and I talked about the wedding until Landon came and whisked her over to be his assistant in a magic trick.

* * *

That night, after another narrow escape from a dream featuring Zach, I paced the bedroom, clutching my cell phone. Goldie watched me from her perch on the edge of the bed, her head resting on Gator between her front paws.

"How much time exactly does a person need to decide whether he's going to forgive a person or not?" I asked Goldie. "I mean, good heavens, it's not like I poisoned him. I was trying to help him. Shouldn't that count for something?" I nodded and crossed my arms as Goldie yawned and rolled over. "You're right. I should just call him. Why am I waiting around for him to call me?"

My heart fluttered in my chest as I waited for it to ring. Right to voicemail. Of course. After all, it was like two in the morning. "Hey, Will, it's me... Darwin. I think it's time we talked and got this sorted out. If you don't ever want to see me again, that's fine but you need to tell me. Not just keep ignoring me. I'm real sorry you feel what I did was wrong. But, I don't." I stopped, shocked I actually said that. And meant it. "So, please call me tomorrow. Good night. Or good morning, because you'll probably get this message in the morning." I hung up before I could ramble on anymore.

CHAPTER TWENTY-EIGHT

Every minute that passed the next day without Will's call was painful. I was exhausted already and the emotional rollercoaster I was putting myself through made the day almost unbearable. By the time lunchtime came around, I was sure we were done. I was angry and fighting back tears even as I helped customers with their purchases.

So, when Will walked through the door, his face drawn and a picnic basket in one hand, I felt a flood of emotions that catapulted me forward into his arms. I didn't care if he was there to dump me. I just had to be in his arms one more time. I pressed my cheek against his powder blue dress shirt and closed my eyes. His free hand came up and caressed the back of my hair, his lips pressed warm against the top of my head.

When I gathered the courage, I looked up into his eyes. They were bright with pain. I wiped at my face and nodded at the basket.

"Lunch?"

"Yeah." He cleared his throat. "Can you get away?"

I glanced back at Willow, who was watching the scene unfold while helping a customer pick out cat food. She nodded, giving me the green light.

"Be right back." I grabbed the blanket from the storage room that I used to sit across the street in the park, told Sylvia I was going to lunch, grabbed my sweater and clipped Goldie's leash on her. "Ready."

The sun warmed our faces as we spread out the blanket on the park lawn.

I watched Will unpack the picnic basket as Goldie stretched out on her belly in the grass beside us and sniffed at a grasshopper. Even though there was plenty of noise from traffic and park-goers, the silence between us was painful. I chewed on the inside of my lip.

"So, what are we having today?"

"Well, for you, a roasted veggie pita." He handed me the wax-paper wrapped sandwich and a bottled water. "And turkey for me." He pulled out an extra wax paper package. "And one fresh butcher bone for Goldie."

I smiled as he offered her the treat and she took it, looking up into his face with a swish of her tail.

"I believe that look was utter adoration," I said, wondering if I give him the same look.

Will glanced at me. He looked like he wanted to say something, but sat back and unwrapped his sandwich instead.

I took a bite and tried to swallow past the lump starting to form in my throat. So, here we were. *What now?* I watched Goldie gnaw happily on her bone. Why couldn't happiness be that simple for humans? I finally swallowed and took a sip of water to wash it down.

"So," I said, trying to sound upbeat and casual, "does this offering mean you've decided to forgive me?"

Will moved his gaze to mine. His eyes were a startling glassy blue, and I tried to shield myself from the assault of intense emotion he was feeling. No one would ever guess this stoic, serious detective felt such a deep well of emotion. He reached for my hand and softly caressed the amethyst ring he had given me. Was he remembering his promise to me the day he put it on my finger? That he would try to keep an open mind.

"I've had a really hard time processing my dad's death, Darwin, and I think all that sadness and anger is getting tangled up with our issues. So, I'm not sure I trust myself or my feelings right now." He brought my hand up to his lips and pressed softly, sighing. His gaze shifted to the distance, and I kept quiet as I waited for him to gather his thoughts. "All I know for sure is I miss you," he said finally.

I blinked back the tears of relief and entangled our fingers together. "I miss you, too."

A genuine smile crinkled the corners of his eyes as he leaned over and gave me a soft kiss. "Finish your sandwich. I've got cherry pie."

I laughed with relief and picked up my sandwich. My heart felt a hundred pounds lighter. "So, congratulations on making an arrest in Victoria's murder. By the way, did the coroner ever figure out how Josie died? Do you think it was those mob guys from Vegas?"

Will chuckled, shaking his head. "You do know that saying curiosity killed the cat, right?" When I just waited, he continued. "All right. Josie died from asphyxiation. There was hemorrhaging around her eyes, bruising around the throat. As for who killed her, no leads yet."

"Asphyxiation?" That was awful. I tried not to picture poor Josie struggling for her last breath. "Well, I learned something interesting from Jade last night. Apparently Josie's dad, Renny, claimed to have a treasure map where some of Jose Gaspar's treasure is buried right here in St. Pete. When I told them about the message Josie left on my phone the night she was killed, Jade's first thought was maybe she found the treasure map in her dad's house."

Will's brow rose. "A pirate treasure map?"

"Yeah, well." I shrugged. "No one's ever seen it, so it's probably just a story he liked to tell to the kids. But what if it's not? That would be motive for someone to murder Josie, right?"

"Yeah, maybe Gasparilla's ghost has come back to claim what's his," he teased.

"Hey, you never know. You heard about the spirit dog spotted at the Pinellas Point Mound, right?"

Will shook his head and took a bite of his sandwich. "Spirit dog, right."

I wanted to tell him about the Native American belief that we all have a guardian spirit but Westerners have lost touch with nature and so their spirit. But, I didn't because there it was... our issue. The one thing that separated us, believing in things unseen. And I didn't want to open up that wound again. I felt a pang of sadness and pushed it away.

I changed the subject. "So, Sylvia has asked me to be her maid of honor. I can't wait to see what kind of dresses Miss Fashionista comes up with."

And so it went as we finished our lunch and enjoyed small talk and each other's company, laughed and had a really good time. But, in the back of my mind, I kept asking myself, *Is this enough?*

Will walked me and Goldie back across Beach Drive. He squeezed my hand as we threaded our way through the tourists to the boutique. "Hey, let's just forget about the whole water thing, okay?" He smiled, brushing my bangs off my forehead.

As I looked into his beautiful blue eyes, my gut clenched and my throat constricted. "Sort of like don't ask, don't tell?"

Will frowned. "Well, I don't want you to hide things from me. We have to be open with each other."

I sighed and let my head drop onto his chest. He pulled me in and hugged me tight. I stayed there for a moment, soaking it in... his touch, his heat, his energy and then pulled away.

"No, Will. We can't forget about it. You need to decide how you feel about it." I reached up and kissed him lightly. "Let me know soon." I walked into the boutique without looking back.

"How'd lunch go?" Willow asked as she watched me unclip Goldie's leash.

I moaned. "I can't say... good, bad. I feel okay, not so desperate and hurt like I was feeling. So, that's good, right?"

Willow smiled. "Yeah, Sis, that's good."

CHAPTER TWENTY-NINE

"So, you do this every Sunday?" Willow asked Frankie, as we helped unload all the pots and trays of breakfast food, plates, cups and other assorted items from the white van. "By yourself?"

"Yes, ma'am." Frankie grunted as she hefted a stock pot onto her hip for transport to the picnic table. "Every Sunday, providing it isn't raining."

Luckily, today was a bright, crisp Sunday morning. I was trying not to think about Josie's funeral later this afternoon. It was too depressing.

"Hey, Mama Maslow," a grinning, scruffy gray-haired man called. "And Snow White. Well, ain't this is a nice surprise. Good to see you."

"Hi, Mac!" I hugged my friend and then motioned for Willow. "This is my sister, Willow. She's visiting from Savannah."

"Nice to meet ya, young lady."

"Likewise." Willow shook his hand and smiled politely.

"Oh, and this is Minnie." I gave the small woman a quick squeeze as she joined us. "I was hoping you were coming today. I've got a couple sweaters for you in the van."

"Thanks." She smiled shyly. "Appreciate it."

"I know you do." I noticed her face appeared swollen and sallow. "Minnie, have you seen a doctor lately? How are you feeling?"

She glanced back at Mac and then shook her head. "I'm all right." She poked a thumb in Mac's direction. "It's that stubborn old horse's behind who needs to see a doctor. He's been having chest pains. I told him to go to the clinic, but he refuses."

"All right. I'll get Frankie to talk to him. You know she won't take no for an answer."

As people came, we filled their plates with scrambled eggs, sausage, donuts, and other treats Frankie had brought. Some of them stayed to chat, others went and sat alone by the lake to eat their food. I noticed another familiar face walking toward us.

"G!" I called, waving like a crazy person. "Hey, G!"

"Hey, Cookie Lady!" He grinned back.

"You sure do have a lot of nicknames here," Willow said, eyeing me curiously as she poured orange juice and handed it to a thin, bearded man I didn't recognize.

"Yeah, I know." I smiled. I actually didn't mind it at all. It made me feel like part of their tribe. I gave G a one-armed hug as his milky eyes glowed in his weathered face. He smelled like bug spray and stale sweat, but I didn't care. "Hey, come on. I got something in the van just for you."

He followed me over to the passenger's side door where I rifled through my straw bag until I found the baggie of lemon cookies.

"Ta da!" I held them in front of him and he promptly slipped them from my fingers with a toothless grin.

"Thank you, nice cookie lady."

"You're welcome, G."

We were walking back to the picnic table when G looked over my shoulder. "Do you have a new dog?"

"Oh," I said, surprised. "Yeah. Her name's Goldie. How did you know?"

He gummed a cookie and pointed behind me. There, behind a tree stood a massive black dog, staring right at me.

I gasped and grabbed G's arm, hurrying him faster toward the table. "That's not my dog, G."

CHAPTER THIRTY

The day had turned overcast as gray clouds bunched up in the sky. The lack of sunshine felt appropriate as a small group began to gather around for Josie's graveside service.

Eugene stood alone in a black suit, his arms stiff, his hands clasped. He looked like he was in physical pain. I made my way over to him.

"Hey, Eugene," I said, trying not to startle him.

He glanced up and nodded. "Darwin. Thanks for coming."

"Well, sure." I let my gaze wander to the coffin. "I didn't know Josie that well, but she had a good heart. She deserves to have her passing mourned." I'm not sure what came over me. Probably that switch in your brain—the one that keeps you from blurting out stupid things—had come undone. But I added, "Hey, I came by your house the other day and saw a woman inside. Dark hair, looked real pretty. I didn't want to bother you, so I left but just wanted to say I'm glad you have a friend to lean on in these difficult times." *What in the name of all that's holy am I doing?* I clamped my mouth shut and froze. Should I apologize for being a snoop?

After a long beat Eugene lifted his head and took a deep breath in, turning to look me right in the face. I met his pale, bloodshot eyes with a forced smile.

"Have you ever lost someone close to you, Darwin?"

"A friend, but not a family member, no," I mumbled.

"Well, let me tell you, it is hell on earth. My wife is never coming home. Ever. My life as I know it is over. So don't judge me."

"Oh." I felt my face burning. "No, I wasn't judging." *Being nosey, yes. Trying to find out who this mystery woman is, yes. Judging, no.*

But I wasn't given a chance to try and squirm my way out of the social gaffe. Eugene had already stepped away from me and went to greet a tall woman in black who had arrived.

I eyed her. Could she be...? Nah, not the woman I saw in Eugene's house. Too tall. *Well, Darwin, that was smooth.* Dropping my head, I slunk back over to stand beside Willow.

"What did you do?" Willow whispered. "You have that same guilty look you had when you broke mom's favorite water pitcher using your magick indoors."

I crossed my arms. "I might have accidently told Eugene I saw that woman in his house."

Willow made a soft sound in her throat. "I'm sure he took that well. You spying on him through the window and all."

I crossed my arms defensively and glanced over at Eugene. "He should try meditation or something. He's a very angry person."

Willow just shook her head as Jade moved to the front of our little group.

I glanced around. It didn't look like Josie had many people who cared about her. Jade was the only one who'd offered to speak. Jade's friend, Sal, stood on the other side of Willow and Frankie, his presence a quiet comfort. Kimi had gone over and stood next to Eugene. I couldn't help but watch them for any sign of a secret affair. The tall woman in the black dress and veiled hat stood stiffly on the other side of Eugene. I wondered if she was a relative.

I had been introduced to the elderly woman in the wheel chair—Josie's Aunt Doris—and her son, who stood dutifully behind his mother with one hand on her chair. And that was it. The culmination of everyone who cared to say goodbye to Josie. I wasn't feeling any overwhelming waves of sadness either, which made me feel even worse.

"Thank you all for coming out today. We all know Josie was a troubled soul," Jade began. "From the time she was a small girl, Renny had his hands full with her. But, she had a good heart and didn't deserve to have her life cut short. Maybe now—" She stopped as her eyes widened and then she cleared her throat.

We all turned to see what she'd been looking at and a mutter went through the small knot of people. Big Barnie was making his way toward us, his head down.

I glanced at Eugene. His face was turning red as a tomato as he clenched his jaw and fists. Definitely could use some anger management tools. Kimi reached out and grabbed his arm as she leaned in and said something to him. The tall woman also laid a hand on his shoulder. Hopefully the two of them could keep his temper in check.

"Maybe now," Jade continued, ignoring Big Barnie as he stood a bit back from everyone, his eyes locked on Josie's casket. "She will find the peace she obviously couldn't find in this life."

Just then there was a scuffle as Eugene broke loose and rushed at Big Barnie. He pushed him hard in the chest, and despite their size difference Barnie actually flew back a few feet. While everyone watched in stunned silence, Jade rushed over and put her small body between them. "Not the time or the place, boys." Her normally quiet voice held power and stopped Eugene's assault.

The woman in black came over and pulled at Eugene's arm. "Come on, sugar, you need to take a walk."

Big Barnie held up his hands. "I just want to pay my respects. She was like family to me, too."

"Family?" Eugene scoffed. "You betrayed our family."

"You shouldn't have come, Barnie," Jade said. "Considering the circumstances of her death." She folded her arms.

"Fine, I'll go," Barnie said. "But I didn't kill Josie. I don't even know how she ended up at my house." He was glaring at Eugene. "Do you?" He shook his head, mumbling something and took the single rose he brought and laid it on the casket before stalking off.

There wasn't much left to the service after that. I said a few words about how I didn't really know Josie that well, but Goldie was always happy to see her and that tells me more about what kind of person she was than anything.

Walking back to our cars, Frankie and Jade talked about the rift between Eugene and Big Barnie.

"So sad. Those two boys grew up together. Barnie was like a son to Renny, too. I don't like seeing Renny's family torn apart like this." Jade's voice was heavy with sadness.

"You think Eugene really believes Barnie killed Josie?" Frankie asked.

Jade shrugged. "By his reaction, I'd say so."

I wasn't so sure his reaction was about Josie at all. Seems the feud I had witnessed between them at Barnie's shop was still going strong.

"Speak of the devil." Frankie nodded toward our cars. Barnie stood there, waiting. We approached him and he held up his hands.

"I'm not here to cause trouble. I just need a word with Jade."

Jade folded her arms. "You can have your word here."

He glanced around at all of us. "All right then. I'm starting to wonder about something, and I was hoping you could help me out. I know Victoria was meeting you the night she was killed to give you something... some artifact she found in Uncle Renny's house. Is that right?"

"Yes."

"Did she tell you what it was?"

"No."

His head dropped and he nodded like he was expecting as much. "All right, thanks."

"What do *you* think it was?" Kimi spoke up.

"I can't say yet. Good day, ladies."

We all watched him walk away.

A niggling itch was tickling my gut. "Can't say? He knows something about Victoria's death. I'm sure of it," I said to no one in particular.

Jade nodded. "Can't say... or won't say?"

CHAPTER THIRTY-ONE

I was letting Frankie in the front door Monday morning just as my phone buzzed in my pocket.

"Come on in." I waved to Frankie, pulling it out and looking at the number. It was Will. My heart soared. "Good morning," I said cheerfully, moving to the tea table. I glanced at Frankie. She looked like she was going to burst with news.

"Morning, Darwin. Listen, I had full intentions of asking you to dinner tonight. I just wanted you to know that. That I want to see you."

"Okay." I glanced at the ceiling. "Something's come up though?"

"Yes. Tara Scarpetta was released last night. Her married boyfriend finally came forward with an alibi for her. The Chief is pissed. We've gotta get back on the Victoria Desoto-Roth case and fix this. I'm really sorry."

My shoulders slumped. "Not your fault. Thanks for calling, Will."

"I'll see you soon. Promise."

"Okay."

We hung up.

"Was that Will?" Frankie squealed. "Did he tell you about Tara being released? Apparently that man we saw her with at the restaurant is her *married* lover. Oh, there's going to be some fireworks in St. Pete today. If all hell don't break loose it'll at least be tugging on its chain!"

I smiled at Frankie and poured some tea. "You seem a little too happy about that."

"Are you kidding! That man is going to be chewed up and spit out by the ladies in this town. And he deserves it."

I put a chocolate éclair on a napkin and licked the cream off my finger. "So, this means Victoria's murderer is still out there." Then I frowned. "Unless Josie did it. That will be harder for Will to prove now."

Willow came from the storage room, and we filled her in on the news about Tara's release.

"What about that woman you saw in Eugene's house? Shouldn't you tell Will about her?"

"I did. I left a message for him the night I saw her, remember? Not sure if he's asked Eugene about it yet. Probably not since he thought the case was solved." I felt my face grow hot as I thought about the funeral when I mentioned her to Eugene. "Maybe they could stake out his house and find out who she is. A secret girlfriend who had access to Victoria's things... including her credit card most likely. That's a pretty strong suspect."

"Whoa, whoa!" Frankie swallowed quickly. "What's this about a secret girlfriend? Was it the woman at the funeral with Eugene? She was a tad overdressed, don't you think?"

I raised a brow at Frankie, glancing at her shiny, leopard print shirt. Talk about the pot calling the kettle black. Gotta love her. "No, the girl I saw at Eugene's was more petite." *About Kimi's height.*

CHAPTER THIRTY-TWO

"No, turn the wheel to the left," Willow instructed patiently.

"Oh, good grief." I hit the brakes and pulled forward again, jerking the car to a stop. "I thought you said this was easy." Shifting into reverse, I turned the wheel to the left and tried to ease my foot down on the gas pedal.

"This is the hardest part. Parallel parking. But, you're going to have to do it to pass the driving test."

"Can't I just memorize all the stuff in the driver's book? I'm much better at that," I whined.

"Sure, if you don't want to ever actually, you know... drive."

"Yeah, yeah."

I'd been practicing driving around the college parking lot for an hour during lunch, and I had been feeling pretty confident until Willow sprung this little gem on me. Parallel parking. What kind of genius invented this? I could feel the sweat under my hairline as my frustration increased. Inhaling deeply, I kept an eye on the driver's side mirror. And... the back tires hit the curb. I growled in frustration, glaring at my sister. Her calmness irritated me.

"Did it take you this long to figure this out?"

She smiled. "Time to head back?"

I put the car in park and unclipped my seat belt. "Yeah. Charlie's great with the customers, but I still feel bad leaving her alone. Thanks for the lesson, though."

"You're welcome. One or two more and you'll be ready to take the test."

I gave her a doubtful look as we switched seats, and Willow drove us back to the parking garage.

The rest of the time flew by. We were all hopped up from the busy day as I locked the boutique door and flipped around the closed sign.

"Charlie, go on home. We can finish up, you've got that big test to study for," I said.

"You sure?" Charlie asked, untangling some leashes on the wall.

"Yeah." I smiled. "Take advantage of Willow helping me while she's here. Go on."

"Thanks."

Sylvia emerged from the back, a few strands of dark hair had fallen from her bun, but she was glowing. "Good night, Charlie. Good luck on your exam." She plopped a fat wedding magazine down on the tea table and waved me over. "Darwin, here, I find the perfect dress for you!"

I shared a smile with Willow as I walked over and looked at where her finger marked. The dress was candy apple red and strapless. Not me at all. But it was all Sylvia. She'd told me her colors would be red and black.

"Well, it's gorgeous." I cocked my hip and motioned to my flat chest. "But, what do you think is going to hold up a strapless dress on me?"

Sylvia waved off my concern. "You'll be fine. It will show off your lovely shoulders." She suddenly looked up. "Oh, Landon, he would like to ask Will to be a groomsman. This is okay with you?"

I knew she was asking if Will and I were okay. Unfortunately, I didn't know. "Yes. They're friends. If he wants Will to be in his wedding party, that's his right. Even if we're not a couple by then."

Sylvia's lips pursed and she gave me a pat on the hand. "Have faith. It will work out how it's supposed to."

I glanced at Willow. She gave me a wry grin. I knew she was thinking the same thing I was. One of Grandma Winters' favorite sayings was, *Have faith, the universe conspires to help you.*

Sylvia flipped open the glossy magazine again. "Anyways, my three cousins will be in these style." She pointed to a dress that had one sleeve with a large flower on one shoulder. "Oh!" She grinned. "And Mage is going to come down the aisle with the rings in a doggie tux. How *precioso,* yes?"

I couldn't help but be affected by her enthusiasm. It was like electricity in the air. I laughed. "Your wedding is going to be amazing."

"Willow, you and your sister must come back in the summer to attend," Sylvia said. "We have decided on August. Slow tourist season. The boutique will not be that busy so we can take a honeymoon."

"I'm sure we can arrange that," Willow said. "Thanks for the invitation."

I smiled at her as I stirred my tea. It would be great to have both my sisters here this summer.

A sudden knock on the window made us all jump. Goldie scrambled up, barking. It was the first time I'd heard her bark. I held my chest as I looked up and then laughed. Jade and Kimi were standing there waving.

Sylvia went and unlocked the door to let them in.

"Hi, we were just passing by on our way to dinner. Do you ladies want to join us?" Jade asked.

"Oh, thanks," I said. "Where are y'all going? We've got some closing up duties to finish but Willow and I can meet you after." I glanced at Willow. She smiled happily.

"We'll be at Cassis," Kimi said. "Mom's hungry for their fish tacos."

"Sounds good. I can bring Goldie then if you sit outside and she can eat dinner, too. They actually have a doggie menu."

"Great, we can do that. It's a nice night. Sylvia, you want to come?"

"No, no, I have to meet Landon. You *senhoras* have fun."

A half an hour later, I was munching on a warm lentil salad, enjoying the stories of Jade's people and what the Spirit Tribe was all about. I was beginning to understand Willow's fascination with their history and belief system, and I loved watching her excitement at hearing the stories. Goldie lay at my feet with her own tasty dinner.

When there was a lull in the conversation, I asked, "So, Jade, y'all have known Eugene and Big Barnie for a long time, right?"

She nodded as she sipped her Pepsi.

"What do you think could cause such a big fight between them? I don't think Eugene was just angry about Josie's death at the funeral."

She and Kimi watched me curiously. "No? Why not?"

I decided to share what I had witnessed. "About two weeks ago, I was in Big Barnie's store and overheard an argument between them in his office. I think Barnie actually punched Eugene because he left with a black eye."

Kimi dropped her fork and stared at me. "So that's where he got the black eye? He wouldn't tell me. What were they saying?"

I tried to remember the exact words. "Eugene had apparently followed Barnie somewhere he was upset about, that made him think Barnie was in love with Victoria... which he didn't deny."

"Her grave, maybe?" Jade said.

I glanced down at my plate. "Could be. Do you think Eugene was right? Do you think Big Barnie was in love with Victoria?" I glanced up at Jade. Her brow was furrowed and she was staring past me, obviously lost in her own thoughts. Kimi had her head down, pushing around the food on her plate.

Finally Jade sighed. "He could have been. But the real question is what made Eugene suspect it suddenly after Victoria's death? And where did Barnie go the night Eugene followed him?"

I shrugged. "Why don't you ask him?"

Jade shook her head. "Big Barnie and I aren't close enough for that kind of conversation. In fact, we've always butted heads. He chooses to make money off our culture instead of respecting it like Renny and Victoria did. No, he wouldn't open up to me."

"What about you, Kimi?" I asked.

"No. He knows I'd take Eugene's side in any argument."

I kept my expression neutral as I nodded and wondered again if she'd been the woman in Victoria's robe that night.

"What about you, Darwin? You could ask him," Jade said.

"Me?" I said in surprise. "I've only had a handful of conversations with him. I don't think he'd talk to me about his personal relationships either. How would I even approach that topic?"

"You could tell him the truth," Willow spoke up. "Tell him we were there at his shop that day and you overheard the argument."

"That might just catch him off guard," Jade said. "Especially if he's been drinking. He has no filter when he's been drinking."

"Oh, I know," Kimi said, getting excited. "Wednesday nights he's always over at Captain's Landing sitting at the bar, sucking down whiskey. You could strike up a conversation with him there and see if he'll talk."

Was that even ethical? I looked over at Willow for some guidance.

She tilted her head sideways and shrugged. "You did say you think he knows something about Victoria's death. And then there's the mystery of Josie's death and her being found at his home. It might be a chance to get some answers."

I bit the inside of my lip and moved my salad around. If I could get some information for Will's murder cases this way, I did have an obligation to try it, right? I wouldn't be putting myself in danger to do it. It was a public place. People would know I was there. "Okay," I said. "I'll do it, but I'm not going alone. We still don't know how Josie ended up at his house. He could have had something to do with her death."

Jade nodded. "All right. We'll all go. They have an outdoor seating deck. We can keep an eye on you from there."

CHAPTER THIRTY-THREE

I brought Frankie with me with instructions to come rescue me a half hour after I started talking to Big Barnie. Figured that'd be enough time to get the information, if I was going to get it.

So, there we were... me, Willow, Jade, Kimi and Frankie seated at a table outside, watching through the window as Big Barnie sucked down his fifth whiskey sour. The large umbrella over our table cut the breeze to make for a pleasantly cool evening.

"Let him get two more in him before you go in," Jade said.

I raised my eyebrows and glanced at the bar. "He'll still be vertical at that point?"

"Yes. And relaxed."

As the others talked, I used the time to reach out and connect with the Bay water to center myself and calm my nerves. I don't know how much time passed before Jade put a warm, dry hand on my arm.

"Okay, the stool just opened up beside him. You're on."

I took a deep breath and nodded. "Wish me luck."

"Luck," they all whispered.

The air conditioning hit me, and I realized I was damp with sweat as I slid onto the bar stool and held up a hand to the bartender. Guess I was more nervous than I realized.

"White wine, please," I said as he approached.

"Hey, I know you." Big Barnie was leaning on the bar, his bloodshot eyes squinting at me. He shook a finger as I just smiled, letting him figure it out. "Yeah, you were at Josie's funeral. How did you know 'er?"

"Oh, hey!" I feigned recognition. "Yeah, you're Barnie, right? I've been to your artifact shop a few times. Great stuff you have in there. So sad about Josie."

The bartender sat my chilled glass in front of me, and I handed him my debit card. "Thank you."

"She was in love with me," he slurred. "Big pain in the rear end, that girl."

I glanced at him, sipping my wine and keeping silent. If he wanted to talk about Josie, I'd let him talk.

"Reckless. Had a death wish. Didn't know when to keep her mouth shut."

Whoa. My heart leapt against my ribs. "Do you think that's what got her killed? Something she said she shouldn't have?"

He moved his gaze to me in slow motion. "How'd you say you knew 'er again?"

I shrugged slightly. He was still pretty sharp for having downed six drinks. "I'm taking care of Victoria's dog, Goldie." I had told him this before, but I didn't think he could access those brain cells in his current state. "Josie came into my boutique to visit her and we just sort of became friends. She had problems, of course, I could tell that, but she also had a good heart. Such a shame her life was cut short like that." I watched him closely. He had his head down, staring into his glass. His hand was clutching the glass tightly, like a life raft.

"Yeah. Goldie. Victoria loved that dog. I remember the joy coming off that woman when they won their first show. First time I saw her really happy."

Okay, we've moved on to Victoria. "That family's seen a lot of tragedy lately. Eugene doesn't seem to be handling it well."

He snorted and downed the rest of his drink in one violent motion. His face darkened at the mention of his friend's name.

"I mean, with the way he attacked you just for coming to Josie's funeral. That just wasn't right." I took a deep breath. *Now or never.* "Oh, or was it something else y'all were fighting about?"

He glanced at me with a storm brewing in those gray eyes. "Why would you ask that?"

"I'm just saying, I would understand." I held his gaze, even though it was making my insides feel like Jell-O. "I was in your shop one day looking for the restroom and overheard y'all fighting in the office. He accused you of being in love with Victoria." I softened my voice to make sure it was sympathetic and not accusatory. "It must have been hard on you, too, if you were... her death."

I sat as still as a rabbit as he stared at me, his jaw working back and forth. Was he deciding if he could trust me, or trying to figure out how he could get rid of me?

Finally, he laughed. Not a happy laugh, but the kind of chuckle that starts as a need for release, way deep down in your gut. I saw tears spring to his eyes, and he broke the staring contest.

"Yeah, I loved her." His voice was full of sadness and whiskey. "She was a great gal. Deserved better."

I let out a breath I didn't realize I was holding and fought the urge to glance out at the table. I knew the gang was watching closely. "Eugene didn't treat her good?"

"He didn't beat her or anything like that. He's just selfish. Always has been. It's all about him."

I sipped my wine as I waited for him to say more. When he didn't, I scrambled for a question to keep him talking. "How did he figure it out now? That you were in love with her?"

He shook his head and motioned for the bartender. "He didn't. Not really. But, he thinks he did. He had the nerve to think bad of her."

"I don't understand," I said after he'd got a refill on his drink.

He sighed, his shoulders slumping. He was getting tired, and I knew my bringing up Victoria was wearing him out emotionally. I strained to hear his next words over the football game playing on three TV's above the bar and the drone of conversations. I think he was actually talking to himself at this point.

"Thinks Victoria shared something with me cause we had a thing. But she didn't. I was just there. At Renny's house. Stopped by to help her out with cleaning out the attic after he died. And to spend time with her. I found a letter he wrote to Jade. Kept it. Something Eugene wants. Maybe we're both selfish bastards. Starting to think it's wrong."

He was slurring bad now. I spotted Frankie heading towards us. Perfect timing, I knew my time was up. Standing up, I placed a comforting hand on his shoulder. "So, Victoria didn't know. That you were in love with her or that you took something out of Renny's house?" It wasn't really a question. I already knew the answer.

He rolled his head back and forth.

As Frankie approached I said, "You should probably go home now, Barnie. I'm going to call you a cab."

CHAPTER THIRTY-FOUR

Friday afternoon, I took the opportunity of a cake delivery close by to give Goldie some exercise. Retrieving my bike from upstairs, I put the boxed cake in the basket and snapped on Goldie's leash.

"Charlie should be in soon," I said to Willow as she helped a customer. "I shouldn't be more than a half hour."

It felt good to stretch my legs, and I could tell Goldie was enjoying the jog. Her head and tail were high in the air as she kept pace with the bike.

We were almost to our destination when, from out of the blue, a white truck with tinted windows crossed two lanes and headed straight for us. I swerved off the sidewalk into someone's yard as I felt the truck skim my leg. I tumbled off the bike, landing hard on my knee, but I made sure I held on to Goldie's leash and yanked her with me off the sidewalk.

"Goldie, here girl," I gasped, as the truck screeched to a halt a few feet away. Goldie ran over and licked my face as I watched an arm pop out of the window and chuck something our way. The truck tires squealed as it took off again.

"Hey, you all right?" A lady was rushing off her porch toward us.

"Yeah, I think so." I winced as I tried to stand. I leaned on Goldie for support and then saw the cake upside down in the grass. *Great.* "More than I can say for Sugar Bear's birthday cake." I pulled out my cell phone to let the client know the cake would be late.

"Crazy drivers around here," the woman said, helping pick my bike up. "Gonna get somebody killed."

I limped over to the object the driver had tossed out the window. It was a brick with a piece of paper held by a rubber band. Unwrapping it, I saw four words in bold type:

MIND YOUR OWN BUSINESS

I limped back over to take my bike from the concerned woman. "Well, at least no one got killed today."

* * *

"What about Tara? Didn't she just get released from jail?"

Willow and I were sitting out on the balcony in the dark, icing my knee and trying to figure out whose hackles I had gotten up.

"Yeah. Could have been her or her married boyfriend, I guess." I winced as I readjusted the icepack. "You know what? I don't want to spend your last bit of time here on this negative stuff." I waggled my eyebrows at her. "Let's talk about our trip to the DMV in the morning." I couldn't believe I was actually going to try to get a driver's license, and that I was more nervous about it than just about anything else I had ever done.

"I guess that's a worthwhile topic." She laughed. "You're not nervous are you?"

"A little."

"You'll do fine."

I pushed my bottom lip out. "Do you really have to leave on Sunday? It's so soon."

"Yes. As exciting as it is here, I need to get back home before mom stresses herself out."

"Well, is there anything else you want to do tomorrow? We have some great museums here."

"No. Maybe visit the Mound one more time. That's more of a museum to me." She smiled. "I need to find a good going away offering. Maybe we can swing by Big Barnie's shop."

"All right, but you're not going alone. Goldie and I are coming with you." I reached down and stroked Goldie's head. "You're a good guard dog, right girl?"

"Yeah right. She'd lick them to death." Willow chuckled and stretched out her legs. "I wish they would catch whoever's digging up the Mound before I leave. I won't be able to fix it from Savannah."

* * *

"Do you want to drive?" Willow grinned and wiggled her keys at me as we exited the DMV after a three-hour ordeal. It felt like leaving a crowded prison.

I was staring at my shiny new Florida driver's license with a mixture of fear and elation.

"Oh my heavens, I can't believe I did it," I squealed, then accepted the keys from Willow and gave her a big hug. "Thanks, Sis. This is seriously the best gift ever! Wait." I dug through my straw bag as we approached her car, finding my cell phone. I snapped a photo of the license and texted it to Will and Frankie with the caption, "I did it!"

Willow glanced at my license photo as she put her seatbelt on. "Could you have grinned any bigger?"

I slipped it into my wallet and started the car. "Nope. I messed up the parallel parking thing the first time, but he let me try again and I did it. And having a sore knee didn't help, but I think the adrenalin overrode the pain. One of the best days of my life." I sighed and checked the mirror as I put the car in reverse. "Where to?"

"For food. Worrying about you makes me hungry."

We spent the afternoon having lunch, shopping and chatting. By the time the light began to change, I felt closer to Willow than I ever had, and I was thanking my guardian stars for this time with her. I was really going to miss her.

"I'm going to go by and pick up Goldie before we head to the Mound. I'm sure she's ready to get out of the house." The light turned green. The traffic still made me nervous, so I accelerated slowly, both hands on the wheel.

"She's probably been sleeping on your bed all day with Gator." Willow laughed.

I decided I really loved driving. The freedom. The control. I couldn't wait to pick out my own car.

As I turned onto the dark street Willow said, "Looks like a party."

There were a dozen cars parked up and down the street. Balloons had been tied to the mailbox across from the Mound. "We'll just have to park down a little ways."

Willow's cell phone buzzed. She glanced at it and shot me a concerned glance. "It's Mallory." She connected the call. "Hey, everything all right?"

I found an open spot along the grass and turned the car off, turning to Willow.

"Oh, okay." She shook her head to let me know everything was fine. "Yeah, I'll tell you all about it. We just got to the Mound. I'm going to visit one last time. You want to talk to Darwin?"

She handed me the phone with a smirk. "She's bored. I'm going to go on up."

I nodded as she picked up the bag with her offering. "Take your time."

"Hey, Mal," I said, grabbing Goldie's leash. She was breathing all over the window, ready for a walk. "I'm glad you called. I wanted to thank you for bringing my chalice when you visited. It's really made a difference in my practice."

"Oh, we're practicing now, are we?" she teased. "Grandma Winters will be happy to hear that."

"Yeah, well. I may have screwed up my relationship with Will with it, but that's a longer story I don't want to get into right now." I opened the back door and clipped on Goldie's leash, letting her jump out of the car. "Oh, hey, guess what I got today?"

"What?"

"My driver's license."

"No way! You too? Did Willow teach you?"

"Yep."

"Well, tell her I'm next when she gets back. Did she tell you mom had a fit about Grandma Winters teaching her?"

"Yeah, she did. You know mom, she's just overprotective." Goldie sniffed at some weeds on the side of the road. I glanced back as headlights swooped over us and then shut off. Back down at the corner of the street, another car had pulled in. "Do you think you can come visit in August? Sylvia and Landon are getting married, and she wanted to invite you and Willow."

"Yeah sure, I wouldn't miss it. That's so great they're getting married."

"It is, and I'm excited about helping her plan. She asked me to be her maid of honor." I squinted at the woman who got out of the car. It was too dark to see anything but her shape as she took something large, like a piece of equipment out of the trunk and headed to the Mound. Her shape and... her long ponytail.

"Hey, Mal, let me call you back in a bit." The hair stood up on my arms as I dialed Will's number and left a message for him where we were and who just showed up.

CHAPTER THIRTY-FIVE

I hurried Goldie back to the car, rolled the windows halfway down for her and quietly made my way back to warn Willow.

Weaving through the wooden entrance gate, I limped along the large privacy fence to the right that separated the Mound from the house next to it. I had to step carefully. It wasn't easy staying quiet while navigating a bed of crushed shells and leaves. When I reached the large banyan tree, I paused, listening over the sounds of nearby traffic and voices drifting in from the party across the street. *Was that beeping coming from on top the Mound?* I had to get closer. There was no way I could climb the hill silently. Plus the leaves were slippery and I had an injured knee. I'd have to take the long way, the path around the Mound and back up. I shooed some gnats away from my face. *Where was Willow?* Creeping through the darkness, I wondered if she had spotted the woman and hid herself.

As I made the slow climb up the slippery, damp backside of the Mound, I definitely heard a metallic beeping. The woman was up there using whatever she had pulled from her trunk. *Is this the mystery woman Eugene is seeing?* If so, she was probably dangerous. *Oh please, Willow, please be hiding.*

My muscles were locking up. Forcing my legs forward a little faster, I ducked behind a large Sabal Palm. I tried to slow my breathing and heart rate. When I got that under control, I peered around the tree. She was here. The machine she swept back and forth emitted high pitched beeping and whining sounds. *Was that a metal detector? Had to be.* I knew any artifacts here were probably pottery or arrowheads made from stone. Nothing a metal detector could pick up. Did she lose something valuable up here then?

My eyes swept the area. Willow was nowhere in sight, though I caught the scent of recently burned sage. Good, she must be staying quiet. I tried to rationalize away my worry. Willow's magick was strong, and she could move the ground beneath this woman's feet if we needed a quick getaway. I squinted, trying to get a better look. She appeared to be taller and thinner than Kimi. *Was it Tara?* Shoot. I couldn't tell. But I didn't think so. This had to be the mystery woman I saw in Eugene's house.

Okay, what now? Should I just pop out and catch her off guard? Or play dumb and act interested in what she's doing? Or should I sneak back to the car and call the police? I wasn't sure she was actually doing anything wrong. My curiosity won. I was about to step out from behind the tree when I heard the shells crunching below. Someone else was coming, and they weren't worried about being quiet. Maybe it was the ghost hunting team? They would have their video camera and could record this woman. That would be a lucky break.

The woman heard them, too. She turned off her metal detector and disappeared behind a tree. Okay, that was suspicious. She was definitely doing something she knew she shouldn't be.

The new visitor was climbing the slippery part of the hill up to the hard ground where we were. It was only one person. I quietly moved around the back of the palm tree, staying out of their line of sight.

After a few moments, a male voice broke through the background noise of distant traffic and the voices drifting in from across the street.

"I'm not exactly sure how to do this but I, um... I wanted to make this right."

I knew that voice! It was Big Barnie.

CHAPTER THIRTY-SIX

I slid around the tree until I could see him in the dim light, sitting on the hard damp ground with something in front of him. *What in heaven's name is he doing here?*

"I've done a terrible thing. I understand now."

A terrible thing? Is he confessing to killing Josie?

"I brought an offering. Of peace. Please, I'm real sorry. I've caused so much pain, and I'm not going to do it again. I'm going to make it right."

As I watched, the woman appeared from behind the tree. She stepped right in front of him. I saw Big Barnie's head tilt up to look at her and then quick as a flash, she swung the metal detector. A sickening crack rang out as Big Barnie fell sideways into the dirt, a yell cut short in his throat.

Without thinking, I scrambled out from behind the tree and jumped on the woman's back. She screeched with surprise.

"Leave him alone!" I screamed in her ear.

With astonishing strength, she flipped me over her shoulder, and I landed with a thud beside Big Barnie. White stars twinkled in my vision and I moaned. My head instantly started throbbing. I tried to grab it, but I was clutching something in my hand. Confusion, pain. I tried to push them aside and sit up.

"Are you all right?" Barnie croaked as he rolled over. A stream of dark blood ran down the side of his face.

I nodded, trying to understand what the scratchy, soft thing I was holding in my hand was. And then the fog lifted from my brain and I gasped. I pushed myself up on one elbow and slowly looked up. *Oh. My. God.* "Eugene?"

"Now look what you've done." He sighed. He had dropped the metal detector and stood clutching a gun, pointing it directly at us. "I tried to warn you to mind your own business."

"That was you who ran me off the road on my bike? Real nice, you could have hurt Goldie, you know... wait—" I moved my attention from him to the wig in my hand. "Oh! That means..." *The woman I saw walking up the stairs in his house... it was actually him.* Then I remembered all the stuff under his bathroom sink. *It was his, not Victoria's. And him answering the door in the silk robe.* "I don't understand."

Barnie stared at the wig in my hand, too. "What the hell, Eugene? You're gay?" he croaked.

"No, I'm not gay, Barnie. Jesus, you think you'd know me better than that. I just enjoy women's clothes."

"A crossdresser?"

Cross dresser? His article! A piece slid into place. *CD faux paus. Cross Dresser faux paus. Wow, was I way off course on that one.*

"Did Victoria know?" I could hear the pain in Big Barnie's voice.

"Yeah, she knew. She just asked I be quiet about it so I didn't embarrass her. I rented cars to go to the club, that sort of thing."

I groaned. *Oh heavens.* "Barnie, sorry to interrupt this little revelation, but I think Eugene has a much bigger secret." I glared up at him. "Did you really do it, Eugene? Kill your own wife?"

His feet shifted around as he sighed. "I didn't mean to," he choked out. "I just wanted to stop her, but I was so full of rage. I couldn't take my foot off the gas pedal. It was like it wasn't even me driving." He sniffed.

Is he crying? I knew the fact he was telling us this was bad news. He didn't plan on letting us leave this Mound alive. He was desperate now. He didn't know my sister was here, though. That was our advantage. I had to get the full story from him while I could. I knew this would be the only chance to learn the truth, while he was in the mood to confess.

"You son of a—" Big Barnie stopped as Eugene leveled the gun right at his head. "Why?"

"Victoria found the copper treasure map Uncle Renny told us about. It's real. He had it hidden in his attic the whole time. But, Victoria said she was going to give it to Jade. Take away our dream of finding the treasure. We had a huge fight about it. But, you knew that already, didn't you? You knew about the map." His voice was shaking. "When I followed you here to the Mound that night and saw you digging, I knew you somehow knew about the map, too. And that you figured out the treasure was buried here. So Victoria must have shown it to you. Why would she do that? Only one reason I can think of." He cocked the gun. "You both betrayed me."

"You idiot!" Barnie roared. "Victoria was always faithful to you. Though you didn't deserve it. She didn't share anything with me. You want to know how I found out about the treasure being here? Fine. I found a letter in Uncle Renny's attic when I was helping Victoria clean. It was addressed to Jade, but I opened it anyway. Uncle Renny was leaving her the map and told her he'd already figured it out, and the Spanish gold's buried right here in this Mound. So, you see, I didn't even need to see the map. Renny said he was leaving it up to her what to do with it. He had kept silent about the treasure buried here all those years out of respect for their culture and for his daughter, Kimi. But, if they needed the money, use it."

"What? Renny was Kimi's father?" *Off the subject, I know. I couldn't help it. I was confused.*

"Yeah," Eugene scoffed. "Good ole Uncle Renny and Jade had a little fling way back. He never got over her. Josie never accepted Kimi as her half-sister, either."

So that's why Kimi had such a strong dislike for Josie.

"Speaking of Josie, you killed her, too, didn't you, Eugene?" Barnie's voice was calm, but I could feel the anger and grief rolling off him. We both waited for an answer.

"Sure, why not?" Eugene's words shot forth like escaping prisoners hell bent on getting over the wall. "You want all the damned details? Why not? Yeah. I let her stay with me and the ungrateful little wench went snooping through my bedroom. She found the map. I heard her leave a message for you that she was bringing it over. I couldn't let her do that. The map's mine. Besides, it's evidence linking me to Victoria's death. I can't go to jail. You understand that right? I wouldn't survive."

Big Barnie pushed himself up off the ground. Eugene backed up a few feet and growled, "Stay right there. I will shoot you."

"I have no doubt," Barnie said sadly. "You've already proven you're a killer. But, Eugene, listen to me. This has to end. I came here tonight to make things right. You can't dig here. This here's sacred ground and there are consequences to disturbing it that you can't even dream of. Worse than prison."

"What are you talking about?" Eugene scoffed. "You've never cared about digging in sacred ground. You just don't want me to find the treasure."

Big Barnie held up his hands. "I'm trying to help you here, Eugene. You and me, we go way back. Beyond this stupid feud over treasure. Okay, I'm going to tell you something that's going to be hard to believe but try to keep an open mind." He glanced at me. "Remember that story in the paper about a ghost hunting team that claimed to see a black spirit dog with red eyes out here on the Mound?"

"No."

"I do." I gingerly pushed myself to stand beside Big Barnie, my head immediately letting me know that was a bad idea. I winced, fighting a spell of dizziness. "I was there and those folks, the ghost hunters, they aren't people who would make something like that up."

"Yeah, well I wouldn't either." Barnie shook his head. "I've been tormented by that spirit dog ever since I started digging here. At first, it was just while I was here. But, last night it came to my home. I woke up, and it was standing over me in bed, those red eyes like fire, teeth white as all get out. It was so real. I could feel its hot breath on my face. I knew it could kill me, spirit or not, and it would if I didn't make amends and put right the damage I did when I disturbed the earth here."

Eugene laughed. "That's a load of crap, Barnie. Nice try, though."

Suddenly, on the slope behind Eugene, I saw movement. My breath caught. Red eyes flashed and then disappeared.

"Holy heaven on a stick, Eugene," I whispered. "I think it's behind you."

"Yeah, like I'm going to fall for that," he said. "Enough talk. Both of you, down on your knees."

CHAPTER THIRTY-SEVEN

"What are you gonna do, shoot us?"

"Yeah. I guess that's the plan. Good thing I have a shovel in my trunk."

"Jesus, Eugene. What happened to you?" Barnie cried.

I winced as my injured knee hit the hard ground. Sweat trickled down my sides as I stared at the gun. *Where the heck is Willow? This would be a great time for her to knock Eugene off his feet.*

"Barnie?" I whispered, starting to panic. Then I saw it again. Two pinpoints of red, to the right of Eugene. Barnie turned his head in that direction. He saw it, too.

A low growl cut through the thick air. It startled Eugene and as he stepped sideways, the gun went off. A flash of light. A crack that sent my ears ringing. Big Barnie jerked backwards. I felt a warm spray on my face and he fell with a thud.

NO!

Everything happened so quickly after that. Eugene's startled cry sounded muffled to my still-ringing ears. He stumbled back, falling and I watched the gun tumble down the slope. He tried to roll after it but something big and dark was suddenly blocking his path.

The spirit dog!

I stood, my legs giving way briefly as my injured knee buckled. I forced them to hold me up. Eugene lay face down in the mixture of crushed shells, leaves and pine needles. He was sobbing. The spirit dog leapt over him and stood in front of me. It was massive. It's head nearly level with mine. *Huh. Big Barnie was right. I can feel the heat from his breath.* And then...

And then I felt a jolt of recognition.

As I stared into the swirling depths of fire that were his eyes... I knew.

"Zach?"

He held my eyes for a moment and then, as car doors slammed and flashlight beams started pushing through the darkness, he simply disappeared.

Boots crunched over the shells. Men yelled, "Police! Don't move!" The Mound suddenly swarmed with light and activity. I couldn't move. I felt frozen in the moment, unable to comprehend what had just happened. It was too much to process.

I felt someone take me into a soft embrace. "It's okay, Sis, you're safe."

I pulled back and looked into Willow's worried eyes.

"Sorry, I left you up here." She stroked the damp hair off my forehead. "I had to sneak away and call the police." She stroked my cheek. "You're bleeding?"

I shook my head. "Not my blood." We watched, arm in arm as paramedics attended to the injured Barnie and officers placed Eugene under arrest.

"He was here." Eugene screeched. "The spirit dog! He's real. Big. Red eyes. Teeth."

"Come on." One of the officers shook his head as he led him down the hill. "We'll get you a psych eval."

Will climbed the hill, his face pale in the artificial light as he approached us. He tried to smile. "We've got to stop meeting like this." He ran a hand over my arm and tilted my face to examine where Eugene's blood had sprayed me. "Are you hurt?"

I shook my head. It pounded and I winced. I pointed to the dark wig on the ground. "That's Eugene's. He killed his wife and Josie." *Why did my voice sound so far away?*

He glanced at the wig and motioned for another officer to come over. Then he nodded at Willow. "Why don't you go ahead and take her down to the ambulance to get checked out. I'll be down in a minute." He pressed a light kiss on my forehead. Something he would never do at a crime scene. *He's worried. I must look real bad.*

As we walked down the soft earth, out to the road, I could hear Goldie barking in the car. *Did she know it was over? Could she sense her mom's murderer had been caught?* I suddenly had the urge to wrap my arms around her.

I glanced up at Willow as she helped walk me around the fence. "Will you get Goldie?"

"Sure." She squeezed my arm and led me through the gathering crowd to the ambulance. "You let them check you over. I'll get her."

I sat on a gurney as gentle, capable hands moved over my body. Goldie rushed out the door as soon as Willow opened it and came bounding down the street to me. Her front paws landed on my chest. She began to lick my face and whine. The warmth of her tongue and spirit began to unthaw my emotions. Tears suddenly sprung up and ran down my face.

"I'm here, girl," I whispered into her fur. I held on to her, burying my face into her neck. "I'm not going anywhere. It's all over."

We gave Will our statements and then I convinced him I was in good enough shape to go rest in my own home. With a last kiss, worried look and a promise to check on me later, he tucked me into Willow's car.

I turned to Willow as she drove us home. "There really was a black dog. Remember Zach, the guy Grandma Winters said sounded like Jinn?"

"Yes?"

"I'm pretty sure it was him. The dog. It was his eyes."

Willow glanced sharply over at me. "From what I've heard about them, they can change shape. Darwin, you don't think he's in love with you, do you?"

My face burned as I recalled the dreams I'd had about him or... with him. "I don't know. Maybe."

"That would be very bad."

"Why?"

"Because one thing I do know is when Jinn fall in love, they become sort of a slave... bound to that person's desires, to help them out in their life. I think that's where the whole genie in a bottle and granting wishes myth came about."

"Well, he's only half Jinn." *But, even as I said it, I knew that didn't matter.* He'd already proven how powerful he was. He could invade my dreams, for heaven sakes. But, a slave to my desires? A flash of being in his arms made me flush deeper. If this was true, this was bad. I had to get him out of my life somehow. But, even as I thought that, I felt a thread of disappointment. I pushed it away. *No.* He was nothing but trouble for me. And Will.

"He knew about me being half water Elemental. He could tell." I rolled my head toward my sister to gauge her reaction. "And he knew about father."

Her eyes slid to mine and then back to the road. "What about father?"

"He knew that he broke the rules with mom, about magick and mortals not being allowed to mix in this dimension. He knew father is imprisoned... somewhere."

Willow's mouth tightened. "Sounds like he's got more than a casual interest in you, Darwin."

Goldie rested her head on the seat beside my head, Gator stuffed firmly in her mouth, and let out a deep sigh. As I turned to give her a cuddle, I saw Willow glance at me with definite fear in her eyes.

"What?" I asked.

"I'm going to stay with you a few extra days."

I rolled my eyes. "Well, I'm glad. But, I hope it's not because you're worried about me. Everything's back to normal now and Zach's gone."

"You don't know that for sure," she said. "Besides, you wouldn't know what normal was if it snuck up and bit you on the behind."

CHAPTER THIRTY-EIGHT

I hugged my knees to my chest. The sand held a chill that leached through the blanket as day began to sink into evening. An empty picnic basket and a few empty wine bottles lay on the beach beside us. We had decided to celebrate on Willow's last evening here. Celebrate Victoria's and Josie's murders being solved, justice being served, new friendships forged, old secrets unburied and well, just life, really. Being alive. Being together.

Big Barnie rested in a beach chair, his arm in a sling. Jade stood beside him, talking as they looked out at the Bay waters. No doubt trying to make sense of all that had happened in their little circle of family and friends.

Willow followed my gaze. "Seems like those two have gotten past their differences."

I nodded. "I think Barnie has made amends. He handed over Renny's letter to her, the one that said Renny was leaving the treasure map to her and Kimi. The police recovered the map from Eugene's house, and Jade's given it to the museum."

"So, they're not going to dig up the Mound for the treasure?"

"No. Not yet, anyway. The archeology department at the University has agreed to take on the project.

They'll use ground penetrating radar to see if anything's there, but it may take years to get the permits to excavate. Anything they find will be of historical value and given to the museum, per Jade's request."

"Guess everything's working out then."

I leveled my gaze past Willow, toward 2nd Avenue. We were on the north side at Spa Beach, right across the street from where Victoria had lost her life. "I guess. Still a shame Victoria and Josie were killed over something that was buried almost 200 years ago."

"Sure is."

Frankie ambled up from the shoreline. "Why are you two looking so serious?" She grinned at us as she pulled her faux fox fur wrap tighter around her shoulders. Itty and Bitty were on her heels, trying to navigate the sand with their tiny paws. "We're supposed to be celebrating."

"Just taking a moment to remember Victoria and Josie," I said, smiling up at my friend. Her red hair had been whipped around by the wind and stuck up every which way, and her eyes were shining. I patted the blanket next to me. A wave of gratitude rushed over me. "Have a seat."

"Oh, I almost forgot," Kimi said from the other side of Willow. She dug through her bag and pulled out a small box. "This is for you, from me and mom."

Willow took the offered box and opened it. "Oh, wow. Kimi, I can't... I can't accept this." She held the clay effigy urn once again. "This should be in a museum."

"And it will be. One day." Kimi smiled gently at

her. "It's been admired in private for a long time, a bit longer won't hurt."

"I don't know what to say," Willow whispered. "Thank you." She gave Kimi a hug and then gently rewrapped the artifact. "I'll take good care of it."

"Oh no, watch out," I said as Goldie came bounding toward us from down the beach, flinging sand, and dropped the soggy tennis ball at my feet. Will had been playing fetch with her for the past twenty minutes.

"Guess she's done with me," Will said as he walked up behind her.

"Okay, that's just nasty, girl." I grimaced, holding the ball between my thumb and middle finger. I tried to chuck it to my left, but it slipped from my fingers and headed straight into the water, making a small plop. Goldie stared at it, her ears forward, then she looked back at me.

"Sorry, girl. I'll get it." I went to push myself up but Goldie suddenly took off. Sand flew off her back feet as they dug in, her tail like a high flag behind her. She bounced right into the water. An audible gasp came from me and Frankie cheered.

"Wahoo! You go, Goldie!" she yelled. "Hey, that's the first time she's gone back in the water, isn't it?"

"Yes," I said, grinning. "Yes, it sure is."

"I'll be."

The gang, knowing the significance of the moment, began to whoop and holler as Goldie trotted back out of the water, her tail whipping back and forth, her head held high.

Itty and Bitty circled her and yipped as she stood over us, dripping, with a silly grin and eyes sparkling. Will came around and sat behind me. I leaned back against him, feeling the sturdiness of his chest and arms as he wrapped them around me, and sighed with contentment as he pressed a kiss on top of my head.

"You and that sunset are all the treasure I need," Will whispered in my ear.

We all laughed as we watched Goldie roll around in the sand, her legs up in the air as she wiggled her rump back and forth, the other pups darting in to jump on her.

There was a moment, as the sky softened from fluorescent orange hues to signal the day's end, and I watched Goldie play with Itty and Bitty, a moment the world seemed to pause and grow silent. And in that moment, on the wind, the words *thank you* were dropped into my ear. I glanced at Willow and Frankie. They didn't seem to hear anything.

"You're welcome," I mouthed, just in case I really wasn't hearing things.

"So," Willow turned to me, "think you can stay out of trouble until we come back for the wedding in August?"

"I don't have a clue why you would ask me that," I said, feigning irritation.

"I have to say, this has been an interesting visit. You sure you don't want to move back home to get away from all the crazy?"

I squeezed Will's arm. "Not a chance."